Ernest Wright

Sea Rhymes

Ernest Wright

Sea Rhymes

ISBN/EAN: 9783337124106

Printed in Europe, USA, Canada, Australia, Japan

Cover: Foto ©Andreas Hilbeck / pixelio.de

More available books at **www.hansebooks.com**

SEA RHYMES

BY

ERNEST WRIGHT

CONTENTS

COMPLETE STORIES

NEW YORK
TROW DIRECTORY, PRINTING AND BOOKBINDING CO.
201-213 EAST TWELFTH STREET
1894

PREFACE

I, THE RHYMER, graduated from the rudest of the
  rabble,
  E'en the Tar, domesticated in a sphere which
    tallies not,
Proficient notwithstanding, nor disqualified to gab-
  ble
  To the courteous a " Salve," *vice versa* " Go to
    pot,"
  Caring little if the others ever notice it or not.

Who stealeth an example thus is innocent of rob-
  bery ;
  So far extremes may meet, it is desirable they
    should ;
Hence " Salve," and the rule is true of egotistic
  snobbery,
  Which, thornlike, crackles audibly, thence " Go
    to pot " is good,
  If awkward, in this weary world of rugged rock
    and mud.

Being crippled in my flippers by a ruling prov-
  idential,
  A dispensation greeted with a philosophic scowl,
Yet having fared famously in every essential,

And deeming gratitude debased by sycophantic
    howl,
I garrulously register my tribute with a growl.

Unabashed by accident, an ignominious glory
    Halowise and misty, o'er the puddle where I
    sink,
And a heart enlarged by humbug, so I meditate a
    story
    Of a chain of circumstances with an odd defec-
    tive link,
    Now seeking prosy utterance by way of printer's
    ink.

If there be any merit, let it fall where it is due,
    On the unseen hand of Providence, from whom
    it surely strayed,
The errors are my property—a legacy to rue,
    My conscience is unhardened by the exercise of
    trade,
    And he who buys may criticise, no matter what
    he paid.

I have an ancient pedigree, for which I see no use,
    And data for events to make a condemnation
    grim ;
That the bilious tongue of misery may wag exceed-
    ing loose,
    Or a wiser brain enlighten with a scientific vim,
    And may Providence enable me to do as much
    for him.

SEA RHYMES

DIGGER'S LUCK

'Twas in Rio de Janeiro, in the year eight-six,
    On board a vessel chartered for the service of
        the mail,
That I found myself, one starry night, where sea-
    men love to mix
    And common fellowship ignores the law of social
        scale,
    Where the fragrance of tobacco adds a gusto to
        the tale.

We were anchored in the centre of that celebrated
        harbor—
    The captain feared the deadly exhalations of the
        town ;
The chief mate and second, with the bo's'n and the
        barber,
    A very decent lot of fellows, hearty, strong, and
        brown,
    After supper gathered forward on the hawser
        flernished down.

There were passengers aboard on the way to
    Buenos Ayres,
      An old Australian digger and a pair from Erin's
      isle;
Alongside in the barges were the niggers working
    near us,
      Rattling and battling, and yelling all the while,
      Who at intervals, in oddly tuneful chorus, drew
      a smile.

The crew were all Norwegian, so of course they
    hung together,
      Apart from where our party talked the prospects
      of the trip,
Made political surmises, or deplored the humid
    weather,
      But no one rose to spin a yarn—the bo's'n had
      the grip,
      And who shall dare to beard the champion liar
      of a ship?

The doctor casually gave a favorable chance,
      By speaking of a queer fish he caught the trip
      before,
Mottled like a leopard; but the oddest circum-
    stance
      Was the finding in its intestines a bit of silver ore,
      For the doctor had dissected it, and sent the
      skin ashore.

The barber said 'twas possible to train a fish for
    profit,
  A notion born of opium, at which we gave a snig-
    ger.
The frosty haired Australian thought very little of
    it,
  But squatting down and smoking in the fashion
    of the digger,
  Proceeded to surround the doctor's story by a
    bigger.

"In eighteen-forty-four," said he, " when mining in
    Australia,
  At Bony Ridge, a settlement of not the best re-
    pute
Its larrikins were desperate, the diggings half a
    failure,
  And citizens who strayed were blest with eye
    and ear acute—
  Night or day the custom of the people was to
    shoot.

" I had quarrelled with my sweetheart, either num-
    ber five or six,
  And feeling lacerated in my vanity or pride,
Had started for the diggings to elude her siren
    tricks,
  Thinking I had seen her worst. Appearance
    must have lied,
  I have sadly found since we were matrimonially
    tied.

" Hustled by the emigrant of every hole and corner
  Of the universe, I hunted up a decent-looking
    chum,
And while we stuck together 'twas unhealthy for
    the scorner,
    And we panned out pretty even, after buying
      bread and rum,
    Likewise, though the life was hard, we revelled in
      it some.

" Mornings, when the head was big, the ocean lay
    quite handy,
So he and I were often in the water for a swim.
His name was Enoch Doxey, just a little of the
    dandy,
    But a thoroughbred in principle, if fashioned
      rather slim,"
    And the old man's voice was husky, and the
      snappy eyes grew dim.

" Those days, a swim was something, for the
    gentleman from China,
    Who ran the little laundry where the public
      wash was done,
Had been accused of leprosy by some impulsive
    miner,
    Who insisted on his treatment with a flourish of
      his gun,
    So they hung him on a gum-tree—he was cured
      in the sun.

" A sailor-boy was Enoch, in a suit of navy blue,
    I was clad in canvas slops, and none too much
        of those ;
We wore them ashore, and when in the water too,
    Which was purifying—none of us possessed a
        change of clothes
    But influential men, and how the cemetery
        knows.

"One morning," he continued, " we were out a fair
        distance,
    Near a lonely rock that jutted up just opposite
        the beach,
    When without a moment's warning or a chance
        to lend assistance,
Poor Enoch disappeared. With a strident,
    chopped-off screech
    I made the rock, a dozen hungry sharks in easy
        reach.

" Darting back and forward, with the dorsal fin
        protruding,
    Or launching downward rapidly and passing out
        of sight,
The number never lessened—they were evidently
        brooding
    On the scurvy trick of which I had been guilty
        in my fright,
    With a grudge against the balker of a healthy
        appetite.

" And, boys, they hung around that rock from
         early morn till dark,
    The torrid sun extracting all the moisture from
         my hide.
I had left my pipe ashore, so I missed the mystic
         spark,
    A fierce thirst consuming me and partially fried,
    Those hungry-looking monsters circling round
         me greeny eyed.

" Night-time came, when moon and stars shed
         down a silver twinkle,
    The ripple of the ocean flashed a million jewels
         back ;
Not a chance to sneak away—an oily, gliding
         wrinkle,
    Where phosphorescent moving patches never
         ceased to wear and tack,
    Like swagmen waiting round a station door for
         their whack.

" Morning came, and all that day I lay without a
         motion—
    I might as well have danced a jig—they never
         moved a jot,
And darkness settled down once more across the
         grand old ocean—
    A phrase which then occurred to me as idiotic
         rot,
    But circumstances often alter phrases, do they
         not ? "

We cheerfully assented, for the yarn was interest-
    ing ;
  The simple-hearted Mac and unsophisticated
    wife
Murmured, " Heaven help his soul !" but nothing
    more protesting,
  We listened to the recital, conjecture running
    rife
  As to how the hardy sinner got ashore with his
    life.

" Again the blazing orb of day sank redly in the
    heavens,
  Midnight came on leaden feet, but lo ! a sudden
    change.
The sharks around my refuge were at sixes or at
    sevens,
  And then I heard our old familiar hail at pistol
    range,
  And Enoch Doxey's face loomed up, but pale
    and somehow strange.

" Whether 'twas the glamour of the moonlight fall-
    ing brightly,
  Or spell of pure madness, I'll not venture to as-
    sert,
But there was Enoch with a nymph, her shoulders
    gleaming whitely,
  Gliding through the wave. She had no bodice
·   to her skirt.
  He was naked, so I said, ' Say, partner, where's
    your shirt ? '

" Ere answering he chose a crevice in the rock that
     suited,
   And placed his silent partner in an attitude of
     ease.
I saw with speechless wonder how the two young
     fools saluted,
   And waddled awkwardly along, as walking on
     their knees,
   And her hair was simply lovely as it floated on
     the breeze.

" She bowed with most bewitching grace and held
     her head erect,
   Waiting while poor Enoch spun the yarn of what
     had passed,
Though after what had happened there was little
     to expect,
   And I beg to state respectfully that I was much
     aghast,
   For their style (or lack) of dress appeared to me
     a little fast.

" Then Enoch said : ' You recollect, I went below
     the water,
   My yell was choked in bubbles as I sank beneath
     the wave,
Where I met with Mrs. Doxey, this young lady,
     Neptune's daughter,
   Who saved me from the sharks in style excep-
     tionally brave,
   And also from the horror of a cold and muddy
     grave.

"'By virtue of hypnotic power she laid me cata-
    leptic;
  All but thought suspended, there I lay upon the
    reef.
Friend, you stare; in such things I also was a
    sceptic.
  All my preconceived ideas came suddenly to
    grief,
  What I've seen these last three days would stag-
    ger all belief.

"'Firstly, she produced a knife of ominous dimen-
    sions,
  Swam beneath a plant nearby, and left me there
    alone,
And when a shark came swimming up with sinister
    intentions,
  She watched it swallow both my legs, and
    crunching flesh and bone,
  Which caused a dull sensation like the crackling
    of stone.

"'When nearly half-devoured, tho' the brute had
    room for more
  The mermaid darted out, and carved away the
    ugly head,
Splicing veins and arteries, suppressed the flow of
    gore,
  Joining all the tendons as they naturally led,
  And sewed the edges neatly, with her hair for
    the thread.

" ' Splitting up the tail, secured a leg in either section,
Which by some healing magnetism grafted very
soon.
Thus I lay for half a day, when, making an inspec-
tion,
She loosed me from my lethargy, a truly welcome boon,
Though I woke in thirty fathoms by the glimmer of the moon.

" ' Another shark who came along, with enterpris-
ing features,
Nibbled speculatively my neck, but she, alert,
Distinguished it forever from its ugly fellow-crea-
tures,
Delivering a vicious cut which evidently hurt,
As it lost no time in leaving, though it tore away
my shirt.

" ' Presently I felt my strength returning by de-
grees,
Nursed with all the lingering devotion of a
mother;
The fish amalgamated with my lacerated knees,
The breathing apparatus worked as well as any
other,
Or otherwise, you know, beneath the water we
should smother.' "

The digger said : " I waded in and felt around the
    junction,
  Altho' his skin was clammy, and I got my
    trousers wet ;
" But there it was, a half-healed ridge," continued
    he with unction ;
  " And Enoch then objected, saying it was tender
    yet,
  So I had to get aboard the rock again, to my re-
    gret.

" ' So,' Enoch said, ' when strong enough to use my
    novel rudders,
  I wandered round and saw the sights, or with
    this lady tarried
(A loose expression which provoked some comfort-
    able shudders),
  Until by love and gratitude our feelings were so
    harried
  That we went to Father Neptune, and were hon-
    orably married.

" ' They wedded us last night, upon a sunken man-
    o'-war—
  A little way due north from here she foundered
    in a blow ;
Her hold is full of canvas bags, and weighty bags
    they are,
  Seized with wire and leaden seals where royal
    markings show,
  But what may be inside them I'll be jiggered if
    I know.'

" He should have said ' be chegoed ' in that vivid
form of speech,
Referring to an insect which, tho' very small
and black,
Adheres to the human epidermis like a leech,
Burrowing beneath it with a diabolic knack,
And leaving some severe inflammation in its
track.

" ' All round the reef and wreck is plenty paying
mud—
I picked a fairish nugget up, and brought it on
for proof.'
Saying which, he passed it out. I found the sample
good,
But when I passed it back to him, he waved his
hand aloof,
And here it is "—the digger passed it out for our
behoof.

" Possibly I dreamed it all, but there is the nugget,
Identically same as that presented by my friend,
If otherwise, I really don't remember when I dug
it,
All our store the night before had come unto an
end—
We generally rioted while dust was there to
spend."

When all had seen the curio, he put it in his
pocket,
Resuming the narration of this singular affair.

(The barber bought it afterwards to make a ladies'
    locket,
    And presented to a widow, with a lover's knot
        in hair.)
    "No doubt of it," the digger said, "I must have
        had it there.

"Enoch told me how they lived, and what they had
    for food,
    Spoke of certain dangers mermaid people should
        avoid,
Told me things I dare not ask for fear of seeming
    rude,
    Which the wife not understanding did not seem
        a whit annoyed,
    And summed up their existence as contentment
        unalloyed.

"'My wife and I,' said he, 'converse by some mag-
    netic lingo,
    Though when we reach the upper air I try to
        teach her this.
I have given her instructions and she's picking up,
    by Jingo!'
    And Enoch looked so radiant with pride and pure
        bliss
    That the pretty little mermaid murmured musi-
        cally, 'Yiss.'

"'We have no money, therefore no treacherous
    rascality,
    No social law, so that we never hear of actions rude;

2

We have no vices, hence remains our unimpaired
    vitality;
    Total lack of dress has banished snob or skinny
      dude,
    And we have the choice of all the sea to forage
      in for food.

" 'And we were on our honeymoon when, struck
    by one idea,
    We changed our course and steered back toward
      this sunken rock,
Put the sharks to death, or flight, discovered you
    were here,
    And shall both be much delighted to escort you
      to the dock,
    If you think your nerves sufficiently recovered
      from the shock.'

" Assisted by the pair of them, I safely swam ashore,
    Where Enoch shook my hand, and said, ' Fare-
      well, my trusty chum,
Unless you should be drowned at sea, we meet
    again no more.'
    But waiting while I rummaged out a hidden jug
      of rum,
    We drank the farewell snifter until grief was
      rendered dumb.

" The last I saw of Enoch, why, he was not griev-
    ing much,
    His bride was towing him to sea, his tails refused
      to crimp ;

In hand he held a trident, trying to use it as a
 crutch,
  As the pain in what were legs produced the feeling of a limp,
  Or impotently jabbing at some inoffensive shrimp.

"Picking up the jug, I started homeward by and by,
  But ere I took the lonely road which led toward
  the tent,
I have no shame to tell you that a tear stood in my
 eye,
  And I took the belts and weapons that were hid
  before we went
  From the ken of prowling biped of felonious intent.

"Indeed my stores had suffered. I had lost a spare
  cloth,
  A powder can had evidently offered up a spoil ;
Things were tossed and tumbled round, which
  made me very wroth
  With tramping scamps who never spin or follow
  honest toil.
  'Tis a mercy to amalgamate such rubbish with
  the soil.

"But I baked the fatted damper, made the tea, and
  broiling meat,
  The way it disappeared would have made your
  steward quail,

Slept like moral justice, which is something rare
    and sweet—
  Remember that I had no sleep when on that
    rocky jail—
  And when I woke 'twas afternoon, and blew a
    living gale.

" Driving down the tent-pegs hard, I sauntered to
    the beach,
  Noticing a drift of spars and rigging there and
    here,
Admiring the shelly growth encrusted thick on
    each—
  Barnacles and oyster-shells, with odd subaqueous
    gear ;
  Evidently deeper growth than any growing near.

" Remembering what Enoch dropped about a sunk-
    en vessel—
  Which Neptune used as chapel or a rendezvous
    for pleasure,
Where mermaid fair or merman bold could gayly
    swim or wrestle,
  With the innocent abandon of unutterable leis-
    ure—
  Whose hold was bunged up to the hatch with
    bloated bags of treasure.

" Here I found a topsail yard, and farther on a gaff,
  A tangled heap of twisted shrouds all thick with
    fossil crust,

The handle of a parasol, which somehow made me
    laugh,
Bolts and iron trappings, eaten badly by the rust,
  The woodwork either petrified or falling into
    dust.

" Presently I saw a plank half hidden by the sand,
  Which once had been elaborately carven, one
    could tell,
Though part of it was battered off by friction with
    the strand.
  There were certain letters in relief, occurring
    parallel,
  Which I puzzled out as ' Bull-dog,' after study
    ing a spell.

" By dint of some exertion, I contrived to hack the
    log,
  Obliterating every mark.   Then, plunging in the
    scrub,
Proceeded to the diggings, where I shot a native
    dog,
  Also a ruffian in my tent, while burgling my tub,
  After filling up his worthless hide with valuable
    grub."

The doctor eyed the digger with an air of interest,
  Remarking that the latter was a questionable
    feat.
But the digger called it justice, and, moreover, of
    the best,

For, he argued, idle bones assist the land to grow
    the wheat
With other necessaries for the workingman to
    eat.

" He never knew what hit him," he continued with
    a grin,
    " And I was only mourner, for I dug his narrow
        bed ;
I searched his pockets, previous to tumbling him
    in,
    When I blundered on a nugget from the grave,
        so that, instead,
    I dropped him down a barren shaft—'twas lucky
        he was dead.

" Poor Enoch ! He and I had suffered many a
    hungry pang,
    As we lay in bed undreaming of the luck be-
        neath the floor ;
And had it been reported now to members of the
    gang,
    My chance of ever profiting was likely to be
        poor,
    Especially as I had helped to wipe out three or
        four.

" Fortune smiled on me that day, for with a single
    pan
    I gathered in more golden pay than for a year
        gone,

Which proves that he who kicks against an evil is
    a man,
  And Providence will see his luck is second unto
    none,
  Providing he survives; if not, we mourn him as
    one.

" Nugget after nugget went to swell my golden
    hoard
  To quite enough to settle on, and live a life of
    ease.
But haunted by the vision of the treasure sunk
    aboard
  Poor Enoch's man-o'-war, I dreamed of more
    than bread and cheese,
  As who would not, whose future promised can-
    vas-back and peas ?

" Later on the pocket failed, so, making for a bank,
  I tried to boom the city with my treasure-hunt-
    ing spec,
Was jeered unanimously as a visionary crank,
  Whose most poetic yarn of mermaids à la bare
    neck
  Was pretty, but improbable as, say, the sunken
    wreck.

" Here I saw my fickle maid, and being reconciled,
  Discovered that a woman may be wonderfully
    dear,
As artful as ' Old Harry,' or as artless as a child,

When she sized up my misfortune with a sym-
    pathetic tear,
And advised me to return to Bony Ridge and
    persevere.

" So, starting in alone, I bought a modern diving
    rig,
    A patent boat, in numbered sections, perfect in
    their fit,
Stores, ammunition, tools, to either build or dig,
    Hiring five adventurers before the party quit,
    With horses and a wagon to convey the heavy
    kit.

" To cross a hundred miles of bush infested by the
    black,
    Armed with spear and waddy, or the mystic
    boomerang,
Which flies in such a manner that it circles whiz-
    zing back,
    And once I followed up its queer gyration with
    a bang,
    Which added one more bogie to the spirits of
    the gang.

" The black believes in spirits, be it ghost or alco-
    holic—
    The latter kind is coveted, the former greatly
    feared—
So after dark he hugs the fire with superstitious
    colic,

And many an angry squatter, when his sheep or
    beef were speared,
Has shot them thus like vermin, till the debt was
    amply cleared.

" A rather curious process is a native liquor-mak-
    ing.
Sooty lubras evolute the grog between their
    jaws,
Which product, when fermented well, would set
    the stomach aching,
If an elephant partook of it ; but not the black's,
    because
His paunch is not amenable to ordinary laws.

" In dietary habit he is subject to vagary,
    The product of the bunya-tree will draw him
    many a mile.
Becoming surfeited thereof, his appetite contrary
    Lets him masticate his enemy, or mutton, with a
    smile—
A Chinaman is reckoned as a remedy for bile.

" No fuss occurred with them this trip ; the num-
    ber of our rifles,
    Or the rollicking revolver as it dangled from the
    belt,
No doubt were marked—they accurately study
    mere trifles—
    For not a man of us received a spear in his pelt,
    Which, lightning-winged and keen, inflict a
    most terrific welt.

" 'Tis a pleasant life, for healthy men to travel in
   the bush,
   Camping out, to sit at night around the ruddy
   blaze,
In perhaps a sheltered hollow, where a crystal
   stream may gush,
   Heaven glowing gorgeously with many-colored
   rays,
   And the breezes fanning coolly, after flaming
   sunny days ;

" An ashcake baking slowly on the embers of the
   fire,
   A kettle odorous of tea, a drop of spirits too,
A rousing yarn delivered by a systematic liar,
   The string upon a tripod twirling steaks of kan-
   garoo,
   A pot of bubbling mutton, or a dainty parrot
   stew ;

" The pipe of variegated hue, whose soothing
   vapor curls
   Around the blissful cranium, evolving many a
   scene
Of bygone happy racket with a varied sort of
   girls,
   And the usual regret—the idiotic might have
   been—
   Unmindful of the torrid heat that withered up
   the green.

" Then slumber deep and holy settles solid o'er the
 camp,
 Like a marble tombstone pinning down a philanthropic screw,
But one lone sentinel awake, to watch for roving
 scamp,
 A brute of gory instinct, with a sight exceeding
  true,
 With arms of modern make, to perforate a sinner
  through.

" Early in the morning, when the skies are paling
 gray,
 The laughing jackass cachinnating diabolic glee,
We rise and hurry breakfast through, and getting
 underway,
 Travel onward till the evening sets the tired
  horses free ;
 In such wise we continued till we came unto the
  sea.

" The diggings were deserted, but the shanties still
 were there,
 A richer find up country had attracted them like
  flies :
Everyone had packed a swag, with little he could
 spare,
 The journey of some ninety miles forbidding
  weight or size,
 Where the peril of the wilderness is naught to
  criticise.

" We confiscated articles to build a roomy shed,
   Fitted up the patent boat, and rigged the diving-
      bell.
After practising a time or two with water over-
      head,
   They mastered all my signals, and were working
      very well,
   Though at first my head felt awkward in the
      narrow copper cell.

" One morning when the day was fine, the ocean
      calm and still,
   We anchored out beyond the rock—the tide was
      nearly low.
I donned the apparatus, and they started up the
      mill,
   Shipped the weight upon my neck and let the
      gunwale go,
   And was lowered down the ladder very carefully
      and slow.

" A certain giddy buzzing seemed to paralyze my
      brain,
   As the pressure from the water drove the blood
      into my head ;
But when my eyes were blest with normal vision
      once again,
   I found myself entangled in a trailing weedy
      bed,
   With myriad forms of ocean life in each direc-
      tion spread.

" Queer plants with scaly arms, which slowly waved
about,
Odd protuberances on the slimy mottled stalk,
Enormous fan-like netted leaves, half petrified, no
doubt;
Underfoot were coral sprays of many branching
fork,
Whose pointed tips were sharp, and made it
dangerous to walk.

" Graceful vines and filaments suspended in the
brine,
Gorgeous bearded flowers palpitating in the tide;
A mellow greenish lustre through the water seemed
to shine
On the colors of a lunar rainbow, much intensi-
fied,
Wavering as silent as a panoramic slide.

" Lovely mosses pendulous on prickle-studded limb,
Glistening bulbs with whiskers, vied with spiny
ball or stump.
I was sunk in admiration, when my eyes grew
oddly dim,
My head began to swim.   I thought, ' A fool is
at the pump!'
Then something hit my helmet front a spirit-jar-
ring thump.

" Looking up, I saw a fish of most unusual size
Tugging like a tiger at the tube that furnished
air,

Which, throbbing to the steady stroke, had caught
    the glassy eye,
    Appearing like an eel perhaps—t'was well it
      didn't tear
    From logic being used unscientifically there.

" I watched my opportunity, it downward swooped
    a little,
    Then drove my dagger deeply in the region of
      the liver,
And much to my relief it wobbled over like a
    skittle,
    In fact, it yielded up the vital spark with scarce
      a quiver,
    Otherwise I might have gone across the fatal
      river.

" Yet felt a bit regretful as I saw the colors fade—
    Golden green and purple streak, or blue and
      crimson tint;
I would have liked the skin, in all those brilliant
    hues arrayed,
    To deck my home when wealthy, that the en-
      vious might squint
    At something unattainable by coin of the mint.

" Solemnly I chopped amid an audience of fishes,
    Who smelt around with more or less desire to
      take a feed.
All but one young shark behaved according to my
    wishes,

Till with the axe I smote him one, which sent
    him off with speed,
Perhaps to fall a victim to another fellow-greed.

" I was struck by the expression of these gentry
    once or twice.
    Their features had a character, as with the hu-
    man race;
Where shrimps appear innocent, and cuttles favor
    vice,
    A white man-eating shark can show a philan-
    thropic face,
    And like philanthropists will need considerable
    space.

" Poor shark! his tender youth was tough; what
    courage he displayed,
    What knack of dodging peril and absorbing
    handy scraps;
How course of time developed it, what social
    mark it made,
    What multitudes have testified, in spite of all
    mishaps,
    Is reverent tradition to the lesser sharks, per-
    haps.

" For when he smiles a toothsome smile between
    his frequent meals
    (Providing nothing happens his ideal will to
    balk),
He plainly looks the generous idea that he feels;

The little fishes view him as the sparrows do a
 hawk,
And have reason to be thankful if the creature
 doesn't talk.

" Nature, wisely vetoing a spurious equality,
 Has fashioned one formidable, another weak and
  small.
Well enough, and even cause for philosophic
 jollity.
 Azrael smites all alike. O Runt, subdue thy gall,
 Cease to grunt and grumble; it is not so hard to
  fall.

" Hacking at the obstacles, I happily emerged
 In a level patch of shelly sand, when near me
  I saw
A wreck careening over, and as eagerly I urged
 My cumbrous way alongside, I recognized it
  for
 The dilapidated relics of an ancient man-o'-war.

" Crusty lichens clustered thick about her copper
  sheath,
 Weedy pennons wabbled from the ragged stump
  of mast;
A yawning cavity exposed the laden hold beneath,
 Where bags, as Enoch had described, were here
  and there cast;
 My mind was in a tumult as I proudly thought,
  'At last!'

" I signalled up at once for rope, and made the end
　.secure
　To a copper bolt projecting from the vessel's
　　battered side ;
Thinking, tho' I knew the place, 'twas better to be
　　sure ;
　Then ascending went aboard the boat, and left
　　a buoy to ride,
　And related my experience with confidential
　　pride.

" The second day was stormy, and the next was
　　even worse,
　A week had passed away without a venture from
　　the land,
And then the bully of the gang informed me, with
　　a curse,
　That they had talked it over and concluded to
　　disband,
　As they were not men to labor for another fel-
　　low's hand.

" When entering this enterprise, they called it rare
　　luck—
　Gambling or worse pursuits had proved a sorry
　　school ;
Now that chance had given them a downy bird to
　　pluck,
　They formed a precious union, according to the
　　rule,
　And honored me, their ' Moses,' with the rôle of
　　dupe or tool.

　3

"A most unpleasant bolus, I absorbed it at a gulp—
　　I meant to get that treasure up, and trust the
　　　rest to fate ;
Alone, I could have pounded anyone of them to
　　　pulp,
　　But seeing odds were heavy, I decided I would
　　　wait,
　　And suggested that he call a meeting to de-
　　　liberate.

" We spoke in solemn council o'er the advent of the
　　find,
　　Swore an oath of brotherhood to share what was
　　　found,
Excepting my expenses, which I thought was very
　　kind,
　　That the treasure-trove was sacred until all was
　　　safe aground,
　　And it somehow struck me then that later on I
　　　might be drowned.

" Of this I never said a word, but in my leisure hour
　　I lined the diving suit with reeding, pliable and
　　　light,
And noting that they looked upon the matter rather
　　sour,
　　Alluded to the sharks and said I baited for a bite,
　　At which remark they laughingly agreed that I
　　　was right.

" Calculating that in case the air-tube should part,
　　The weight of water naturally pressing to the skin

Would clog whatever effort I could manage from
    the start,
  Where the suit distended thus would stop the
    water pressing in,
And counteract the gravity of leaded moccasin.

" It worked a little stiff at first about the arms and
    knees,
  But showed a great improvement after using
    once or twice ;
And presently I learned to move about in it with
    ease,
  Never losing any chance to pad or perfect my
    device,
  Considering my safety very cheap at such a price.

Not being apprehensive yet, for I was sure of this,
  No member cared to risk his precious life below
    the wave,
But had a strong suspicion that affairs would go
    amiss
  When the booty was recovered from its tem-
    porary grave ;
So I stowed a lot of stuff away, unnoticed, in a
    cave,

" The same that I and Enoch used in days, alas !
    gone by ;
  'Twas there we left our weapons ere that final,
    fatal swim."
And the old man paused a moment to project a
    heavy sigh,

Then continued: " No one knew of it, excepting
    I and him,
And I had kept it secret from the prompting of a
    whim.

" A can or two of powder and some weapons disap-
    peared ;
No one made remarks, it was not safe to cogitate,
Communities become polite when treachery is
    feared ;
Everybody's firearms were fully up to date,
In case enthusiasm got the better of debate.

" In course of time the weather cleared, the sea was
    smooth as glass,
We pulled out to the vessel, dropping anchor by
    the buoy ;
So down I confidently went.   It also came to pass
    That after sending up a load, I signalled ' Boat
    ahoy ! '
    And found the blessed mob of them delirious
    with joy.

" Some proposed to open one, to make the matter
    sure,
    The rest were very certain that for such a bulk,
    the weight
Was surely gold or silver, may be dust, but very
    pure ;
    So we buried all unopened with the digger's
    handy sleight,
    And started out again to get another precious
    freight.

" I came across a turtle poking round among the
     weed,
  Stirring up the sand in quite an animated style,
Got a fair slanting cut, it paying little heed,
  Beheading it, altho' the flippers twitched a fair
     while
  After being hauled up in the boat to swell the
     dinner pile

" Whereby I nearly lost my life. The flavor of the
     flesh,
  Spreading through the current, advertising far
     and wide,
Allured a monster devil-fish (they like their rations
     fresh),
  Which with horrible contortions straggled sway-
     ing thro' the tide,
  And chased me in the hold, where luck enabled
     me to hide

" In a locker, near a barrelful of navy pickle beef,
  Which it tackled in a fury, squeezing in the oaken
     stave,
And tho' 'twas over average, the creature came to
     grief,
  For it swallowed down a morsel, then a frightful
     shudder gave,
  And, collapsing, died. I also had a rather narrow
     shave.

" Whether 'twas the pickle or the toughness of the
     meat,
  Being unimaginative, I must let the doctor judge;

I opened out the stomach, found the fatal bit com-
    plete,
    And a pair of leather pantaloons, digested into
      smudge,
    So I came to the conclusion that it owed itself a
      grudge.

" And having nerves, I told the men a tale about the
    mould,
    Or sand, by lapse of time accumulated in the
      claim,
Requiring time and labor to remove it from the
    hold.
    I took a pick and shovel to substantiate the game,
    But started on a tour round the vessel just the
      same.

"Laying off the leaden weight upon the helmet rim
    Enabled me to rise at will by paying out a cord,
Then hauling up the weight thereby and placing it
    in trim ;
    I stood upon the upper deck for years unex-
      plored,
    Without the people in the boat assisting me
      aboard.

" Her starboard rail· was shattered in some bygone
    heavy gale,
    The port side entire, which, inclining by the slant,
Had banked the scuppers up with sand to level
    with the rail,

And made a level promenade, unchoked by ocean
    plant,
Which every here and there sprouted up luxuri-
    ant.

" Fallen from the carriage lay the ancient carro-
    nade,
    Never more to vomit death or cripples at the
      foe ;
Shot stood in the racks, from which the lashings
    had decayed,
    And silent now the voice which used to bellow
      ' Let her go ! '
    But oh ! it was a dandy place for barnacles to
      grow.

" The pins were rusted in the rail, where hung the
    ragged shred
    Of fossil rope, existing yet from countless coats
      of tar.
Here I found a square cake of common navy bread,
    In which the water had not penetrated very far,
    Which testifies to what substantial edibles they
      are.

" The deck was clear fore and aft, from where the
    foc's'le rose
    Away unto the quarterdeck, and poop of fair
      height,
Beneath which was the armory, and cabins, I sup-
    pose,

For the non-commissioned officers, whose lot in
     life was bright
If they had a cuddy large enough to shelter in
     at night.

" Here were arms of ancient make, all swollen up
     with rust,
     Boarding pikes, and cutlasses resembling pagan
       clubs;
A skylight on the quarterdeck was darkened by a
     crust,
     While nearby a double wheel had rotted to the
       hubs,
     And looked unspoken havoc through a double
       row of stubs.

" Hairy bordered jelly-fishes, wallowing the stream,
     Shells were crawling o'er the deck, of varied
       shape and hue,
Richly stained and polished, or with iridescent
     gleam.
     Then I spied a bed of oysters, gaping juicy
       where they grew,
     And my soul was sublimated by a dream of oys-
       ter stew.

" Stepping down the midship hatch, I did not
     travel far
     Ere on the captain's cabin floor I found a set of
       bones,

A casket in its fingers made of carven fluorspar,
   Containing, as I ascertained, some valuable stones,
   Which the skeleton had grabbed before it went
      to Davy Jones.

" 'Twas food for speculation what these relics
      might have been,
   In that proud, imperial period, a British captain's
      life.
So picking up the skull I tried to conjure up the
      scene,
   But a dozen rusty hairpins proved it must have
      been the wife ;
   There lay also ruby eardrops and a slender silver
      knife.

" The captain's bones I shortly found, asprawl upon
      a bunk,
   A broken flask lay near, once containing rum, I
      think ;
A liberal grin suggested that he died extremely
      drunk.
   The sockets seemed to flicker with a double-bar-
      relled wink,
   And a bony arm extended, as declining more to
      drink.

" A sorry-looking spectacle—the table dropped
      apart,
   Furniture decayed or lying sodden on the floor,
Slimy ooze and weeds upon the panels once so
      smart ;

Water running riot in the place of rare store,
And a merry mob consuming, with an appetite
  for more.

" Nearer to the port stood a rusty iron chest,
  Large enough to hold a man, but tightly shut
    and locked,
And when I loosened up an end, by way of making
    test
  Of the weight contained therein, it flew up over-
    head and knocked,
  As I pried away the fastening by which it had
    been chocked.

"Consideration proved the cause—the chest was
    airtight,
  And being firmly wedged unto the deck could
    never shift.
Presently I found two money lockers, not so light,
  So lashing all together so that none would go
    adrift,
  I launched them through the stern port by a
    herculean lift.

" Another day I lugged them out between the ship
    and grove,
  Took a line and lashed the heavy specie to an
    end,
The balance of the rope through both the iron
    handles rove,

Kept the chest suspended upright, anchored
 firmly by a bend
That would slip and run, according as required
 to ascend.

" Returning to the forward part, I stove the fore
 hatch,
 Descended crazy iron steps, and lo! the home of
 ' Jack,'
With hammocks scattered o'er the deck in sodden
 muddy batch,
 The bony parts of skeletons protruding from the
 wrack,
 Like relics of some murderous piratical attack.

" She met her fate at midnight, it was easy to be
 seen
 From a batch of stony firewood in the for'a'd
 galley grate;
The coppers both were empty, and were turned a
 dirty green.
 Then I left the seamen's quarters, as the time was
 growing late,
 By the ladder, which was in a most dilapidated
 state.

" Returning to the breach below, I loaded up again,
 The last we took ashore that day. My chest
 was growing weak,
Heavy breathing warned me of too long-continued
 strain,

And in the upper air I found it difficult to speak,
From odd sensations in the lungs, as if they'd
    sprung a leak.

" Working every day, except an accidental spell
    On squally days, or when the gang were danger-
    ous with grog—
Times I never went below, I dare not, truth to tell—
    For no one man could fairly work a pump and
    dance a clog,
    Which hits the insane humor of the jolly drunken
    dog.

" On first investigation of the sunken vessel's hold,
    I stumbled on a barrelful of rare old oily rum,
And sent it up, incautiously—the sequel I have
    told—
    With a score or two of rotten-looking cases,
    wherefrom
    Handy bottles of the fluid seemed to magically
    come.

" Time brings all things to an end, and so the cargo
    sank,
    Till naught remained of it but scarce a comfort-
    able load.
The company grew surlier, and muttered of the
    bank,
    Or the surplus which was due to me according
    to our code,
    And also of the time when we should all be on
    the road.

" 'Twas evening, but they urged that I should finish
    up the job,
  So that to-morrow we could rest, and portion out
    the spoil ;
And on due consideration this idea of the mob
  Was adopted, and I willingly returned below to
    toil,
  For the darkness would befriend me in the case
    of any broil.

" Leisurely the bags went up, till there remained but
    one,
  And that went too. And then I gave the signal,
    ' Finished work.'
Instead of being hoisted up I found the air gone,
  The anchor hoisted hurriedly with frantic, hasty
    jerk ;
  The tube and line were severed by a hatchet or
    a dirk.

" All this went rushing through my mind more rapid
    than a flash.
  I cut the tube and stoppered it—the valves were
    water-tight,
(I signalled from the chest, ' Hooked on '), and,
    steadied by the cash,
  I paid the line out quickly, till I saw a starry
    light,
  Then took the helmet grating out, and found my-
    self all right.

"Keeping well submerged, I kept the buoy before
  my head,
 Dimly saw them pull ashore, and land the precious stock,
Apparently not dreaming that their victim was not
  dead,
 Then buoyed the line, and got the floating chest
  on to the rock,
 Fastening the painter to an upward jutting block.

"And when I saw their camp-fire flaring out upon
  the land,
 I stripped, and swam ashore, with the rig and
  chest along,
Which I hid with weed and wreckage in an inlet of
  the sand,
 Visited the cavern, but discovered nothing
  wrong,
 Donned another suit, and took a nip of something
  strong,

"Not omitting sundry weapons, ere I made a furtive
  scout—
 The gang had every reason to resent my scurvy
  trick,
And doubtless they would do their best to wipe a
  fellow out.
 So I travelled very carefully, avoiding every
  stick,
 But progressing through the bushes in a manner
  very slick.

" Their camp lay in a hollow, by a little trickling
    rill ;
  A rock ran parallel with it, and bushes on the
    top
Made a cover for a fair view.   The air being still
  Transmitted very clearly any word they chanced
    to drop,
  And the tableau they presented would have
    shamed a liquor-shop.

" Seated in a circle round a bonny blazing fire,
  Pannikins were passing from a bucketful of rum,
Their bloodshot vision leering with a maniac de-
    sire
  On a treasure-bag, all eager for whatever was to
    come,
  While their leader held a chisel 'twixt a finger
    and a thumb.

" Carefully he cut the wire and dropped the leaden
    seal,
  Opened out the brittle bag by one impatient rip.
A solid earthen jar appeared, on which the busy
    steel,
  Wielded by the Judas of the gang, began to clip,
  For the lid was well cemented to a wide project-
    ing lip.

" Fiercer glared the eyeballs of those ruffians in the
    bush,
  Excitement lent a tragic mien to features coarsely
    gruff,

Then click! the lid flew off at last, amid a breathless
    hush,
    And plump, upon the floor, full among the worth-
      less stuff,
    Fell a heavy blackened sample of an English
      Christmas duff.

" Then spoke the burly villain, but in strangely al-
    tered tones,
    Saying, ' Partners, this is mermaid craft,' and as
      they all were tight
None objected to the theory. ' And now,' said he,
    ' the bones
    Of the boss, with all our wages, are at Davy
      Jones' to-night,'
    Then took another tot of rum, and staggered out
      of sight.

" Aghast, they stared, ' the horror of a brutalized
    despair,'
    Till someone broke the silence by remarking,
      ' 'Twas a spell.
Our leader engineered that evil business over there.
    Now he is drunk and sleeping, therefore easier
      to quell,
    I vote we execute him.' And they took it very
      well.

" For they put a bullet through the modern Jonah
    of the crew,
    Then opened half a dozen bags, but found no
      other change.

So, being greatly mystified, and feeling rather blue,
  For the advent of the puddings was unnaturally
    strange,
  I very quietly wriggled off, and soon was out of
    range.

"And feeling pretty sure none would track my
    careful feet,
  I brought provisions out, and lit a fire in the
    grot—
A damper and a can of tea, a rare cut of meat
  From a kangaroo in splendid form which I had
    lately shot,
  Anticipating that affairs were getting rather hot.

" Shaking out a truss of twigs, a blanket neatly
    spread,
  I soon was sleeping soundly by the fire's fitful
    gleam ;
But echoes of the late events came trooping
    through my head
  With a strain of disappointment like a sorrowful
    requiem,
  Till I found myself below the wave—of course,
    in a dream.

" I dreamt I slew a devil-fish, and severed all the
    limbs
  With the jawbone of a sailor, when I had an
    awful scare.
The genuine sea-serpent which was seen by Cap-
    tain Sims,

4

Having scented gore, came rushing like a cy-
　　clone from its lair,
Its eyeballs coruscating with a most unpleasant
　　glare.

"And it happened in my vision, being near the
　　sunken craft,
　By some severe exertion up I scrambled through
　　　a port,
And sinking down beside a gun, hysterically laughed
　While the monster twined his scaly length in
　　　diabolic sort,
　Or clashed his jaws and snapped in truly vicious-
　　looking sport.

"Then a narwhal, with a rushing swish of water,
　　keenly flashed
　From the jungle patch of seaweed like an arrow
　　from the bow,
A spiral ivory tusk into the reptile body crashed ;
　Mud and sand arose in clouds, dissolved by dire
　　throe,
　And they vanished, locked together—I rejoiced
　　to see them go.

"Looking round the deck, which was phenome-
　　nally clean
And level as the surface of a board newly planed,
An inspiration struck me that it probably had been
　Neptune's private ball-room, which my presence
　　had profaned,
　Polished up with scaly tails and curiously
　　grained.

" And even while I cowered in my shelter by the
       gun
  Neptune sailed majestically by me with his
       crew.
I knelt in mortal terror, yet I quite enjoyed the
       fun.
  They paired off in couples as the folks ashore
       do,
  But the queer gyrating figures of the dance to
       me were new.

" Neptune waved a measure with a trident held
       aloft,
  A bushy-bearded merman swung a nymph in
       giddy whirl,
Her features quite transfigured by a look so coy
       and soft,
  And my heart went like a hammer when he
       kissed his chosen girl,
  But as couple followed couple, why, it made my
       hair curl.

" Anchors, hearts, and arrows, worked in red and
       purple stain,
  Were tattooed on each bare arm or bosom of the
       male,
' Sailors of the Bull-dog come to visit her again ;
  The watch on deck, most probably,' I thought,
     ' could tell a tale
  Of the sinking with their vessel in that long-for-
       gotten gale.'

" If not, they were as lively as the tars before the
        mast
    Can hardly fail to be when there's a woman in
        the case.
I watched the curious revel out, and when they
        glided past
    A happy look was patent on each rugged sailor
        face,
    While the mermaids were the essence of a culti-
        vated grace.

" Neptune, with his massive limbs and noble figure-
        head,
    Left a whirling wake of water to the rear as he
        progressed
With Amphytrite, his fair queen, although her hair
        was red,
    And decency would recommend that ladies
        should be dressed ;
    Yet the beauty of her figure really cannot be
        expressed.

" Her tail came into contact with the rusty tube of
        iron,
    A subtle living magnetism gave me quite a
        shock.
The next I knew, a rumble like the roar of a lion,
    A belching flame, a flight, a fall, a fearful heavy
        knock—
    I woke—to find I'd fallen off the bed upon the
        rock.

"'That blessed gun was loaded,' I remarked unto
  myself,
  While scrambling half mechanically back upon
  the bed,
Where, sinking into slumber, all my worry on the
  shelf,
  My sleep remained as peaceful, also dreamless,
  as the dead,
  And when I woke the sun was shining brightly
  overhead.

" I visited the other camp, supposing all asleep
  In the lethargy of drunkenness, as often happed
  of yore,
And crawling to the parapet, I stole a furtive
  peep,
  But stared, for the site was now a cellar, littered
  o'er
  With broken bits of wreckage, but the shanty
  was no more.

" An open keg of powder in the stores had been
  fired,
  Which promptly paid the compliment by firing
  everything ;
The gang were blown to atoms, with a finish I
  admired,
  Save one—as blind as forty bats, not mentioning
  the sting,
  Which must have been most exquisite, to hear
  the beggar sing.

"He thought he was in Hades when he heard my
    well-known voice ;
When undeceived, he fell into a pitiable fright.
I was more inclined to pity his misfortune than re-
    joice
    When he told me of the tragedy that took away
    his sight,
    The shock of which inspired my dream and
    tumble in the night.

"I bandaged up the caverns where his eyes were
    wont to shine
    With tepid tea and cotton, which appeared to
    give him ease,
Thanked my lucky stars I had the proper use of
    mine ;
    As I led him home, I found him, crawling on his
    hands and knees,
    By the rivulet, and bumping on the rockery and
    trees.

"They healed up very slowly ; it was after many a
    day
    That he went out to the buoy with me, assisting
    in the scow,
When we hauled up both the boxes in a clumsy
    kind of way,
    And floated them ashore, half suspended from the
    bow,
    With a bag of keys and trinkets unavailable till
    now.

" We drew the chest up on the beach and chose a
    likely key,
  Punched a brazen plate along the closely fitting
    slide,
And found the lock uninjured, for the end was
    entered free ;
  We turned it over twice before it shot the bolt
    aside,
  Then we hammered on the hinges till the cover
    opened wide.

" Whatever we expected I am sure I forget,
  As I recollect the items of that queer fricas-
    see—
A wreck of satin wedding-dress, some ornaments
    of jet,
  A diamond necklace, rubies set in tarnished
    filigree,
  Discolored by long sojourn at the bottom of the
    sea.

" The chest had once been fitted up with neatly
    fashioned trays,
  In which were jumbled yellow lace of pattern old
    and rare,
With sundry foreign notions worked in most ec-
    centric ways,
  Documents, and human fads, for which I did not
    care,
  Though certainly I wondered at a pad of musty
    hair.

" I picked a dainty missive up at random from the
    pile,
  Worded most effusively, with crest of some pre-
    tence,
Congratulating someone in aristocratic style
  On his marriage with a fair dame of rank and
    consequence,
  With felicitous allusions to the crowding and ex-
    pense.

" The date was hardly legible, 'twas seventeen
    something else,
  So I took another paper up, and scanned the
    faded lines,
Which related to the trading of some valuable pelts,
  A note of smuggled spirits, and a list of foreign
    wines,
  With a pamphlet on the scientific management of
    mines.

" Next a parchment, decked with royal arms and
    private seal,
  Of his majesty King George the Third, appoint-
    ing from the date,
To the sailing-vessel Bull-dog, for the British com-
    monweal,
  Sir William—I forget his name—to rule subordi-
    nate
  And administer according to the dictum of the
    state.

"'Twill be seen in English history of a hundred
    years back
  That George the Third was born and educated
    on the soil.
He married well and wisely, and pursued a pru-
    dent track,
  So Whig and Tory patriot deferred politic
    broil,
  And burnt a common fire to make the royal
    kettle boil.

" The nation bubbled over with enthusiastic zeal
  At the gorgeous coronation of this paragon of
    ' kings ;
Then a certain class of sentimental cranks began to
    feel
  For the misery of murderers and prison scatter-
    lings,
  And formed a club to furnish them with fruit
    and diamond rings.

" Not native vagabonds, or those whose trespasses
    were venial—
  Such vermin were neglected, being little under-
    stood,
Charity at home was relegated to the menial,
  Who pampered the policeman of the near neigh-
    borhood,
  And generally succored all the relatives she
    could.

" Perhaps a holy nimbus hung around the vicious
            brute
    Whose liberty was forfeited by every just de-
        cree ;
Or the great reforming remedy was jewelry and
            fruit,
    But the charity hysterical, however that may be,
    Grotesquely boomed the project with a philan-
        thropic glee.

" Missionary meetings furnished subsidies of cash,
    Private generosity contributed as well—
If any doubter sneered, he was stigmatized as rash ;
    In short, it was the fashion, and to borrow, beg,
        or sell
    For the benefit of rascaldom was reckoned very
        swell.

" And when each worthy manager had fingered o'er
            the heap,
    'Twas found that diamonds were too dear for
        such a modest sum,
So that twenty thousand puddings (made and
            neatly packed to keep)
    Were given for the hardened of colonial prison
        scum,
    Each present supplemented by a flask of pure
        rum.

" Parliament, influenced by petitions and the like,
    Put the Bull-dog in commission for the carriage
        of the stuff,

And when she sailed away the captain, happening
    to strike
  A case of spirits, broken when the sea was rather
    rough,
  Took to sampling the liquor, but he never touched
    the duff.

" Being unfit to navigate the vessel up the coast,
  The officer in charge, half drunk or taking little
    note,
No matter if the sailor was on duty at his post,
  They struck the digger's rock, which pierced the
    bottom of the boat,
  Then drifting onward foundered—and the pud-
    dings wouldn't float.

" This I gathered mostly from the log-book in the
    chest.
  The captain's bride was spoken of no more than
    I have told ;
The boxes held the sailors' pay, and money for the
    rest
  Of a man-o'-war's expenses, which are simply
    manifold.
  There was eighty pounds in silver, thirty thou-
    sand more in gold.

" I have very little more to add, excepting that a
    boom
  Occurred in Bony Ridge again. The diggers
    came like geese.
I hid away the money, built a shed with plenty room,

In which I stowed the bags.   My luck continued
    to increase ;
I sold the lot, and averaged a sovereign apiece,

" Then got my stuff together, joined a city caravan,
    Got there in a week.   The jewels found a ready
      sale.
Married there, and settled down, a fairly wealthy
    man.
    I travel now for pleasure when the colonies are
      stale."
    And that's about the finish of the digger's queer
      tale.

He rose, and slowly ambled somewhat stiffly down
    below.
    We sat and watched him vanish like the ghost of
      Ananias.
The bo's'n never afterward was quite so apt to
    crow ;
    The Irishman and wife ejaculated something
      pious,
    Being mentally constructed on a sympathetic
      bias.

The first and second mate pronounced the story
    pretty stiff ;
    The steward swore profanely that a mermaid was
      a fact,
Had seen one in a quicksand from a certain lofty
    cliff,

But admitted, when bedazzled by the doctor's
    subtle tact,
That it happened on a pay night after many
    bottles cracked.

The doctor's verdict on the yarn was plausible
    enough.
A psychologic trance was indicated as the cause
Of Enoch's resurrection, and the finding of the duff,
    Unconscious action of the brain, obeying certain
    laws,
    Evolved, perhaps, by instinct operating on the
    jaws.

In other words, insanity induced by dire thirst
    Had conjured up the mermaid scene, and lent a
    nerve to dare.
Luck attended his escape, but having swallowed
    first
    A draught of old Jamaica while delirium lingered
    there,
    A monomania governed his ideas unaware.

For curious coincidence of dream or omen proved,
    He cited from the lotteries, where numbers came
    out true,
Visions haunting murderers, and brothers oddly
    moved,
    Tho' many miles apart, if harm hit either of the
    two,
    And of accident occurring after people feeling
    blue.

The barber said he didn't know, and there he told
    the truth—
  He used a deal of opium, poor fool; his face was
    white,
And his wit at times was stupid, though the poor
    misguided youth
  Had not slit a throat, or shown the least pro-
    clivity to bite.
  So they let him shave the passengers, in case he
    some day might.

The bo's'n and the rest departed, each unto his
    berth,
  While the night relay of niggers did their best to
    murder sleep.
And now I've written out the yarn for what it may
    be worth,
  As a specimen of stories told upon the briny deep,
  And wondering if, like the digger's puddings, it
    will keep.

HONEYWELLS. A RHYMER'S TALE.*

INTRODUCTION.

EXISTENCE is at best a muddy liquor,
  Drunk with somewhat varying effect;
Some eternally inclined to bicker,
  While others pose as being the elect;
Another blunders on, a chronic kicker,
  Or mouches by with moral feeling wreck'd,
Whereat the learned jibe, yet know no quicker,
  In spite of a superior intellect,
The ultimatum of a speculation
Beyond the grave, or happily—cremation.

Eccentric in detail, the system jogs,
  Some labor, others may manipulate
The subtle tricks of trade, as needful cogs,
  On wheels that whirl in manner intricate;
So branches, leaves, and twigs, ere heavy logs
  Are fashioned in a ship to navigate.
Here and there I notice men or dogs
  Are valued for their pedigree, a state
Of things endured by the toiling crowd,
And animals who cannot think aloud.

* NOTICE.—All names used in this story are fictitious.

Labor to the strong may rival leisure,
   And in necessity a merit lies ;
The rich and poor enjoy in equal measure
   Their raiment, provender, or exercise ;
Peril mingles in with garnered treasure,
   Invisible to ordinary eyes.
There is a limit unto every pleasure,
   Excess is certain to demoralize.
Habit dominates ideal sense,
Even when improved at great expense.

The human soul is rather hard to please,
   'Tis somewhat prone to avaricious greed ;
Yet God is just to even selfish ease,
   The chief initial cause of squalid need,
Whose feeble ranks perpetuate disease,
   Prolific in a germinative seed,
Which travel on the breeze where It may please ;
   And where those atoms find a home, they breed
The ignorant, the wise, the foul and fair
Exchange ideas through one common air.

To hamper wrong enormous sums are spent,
   Religion sells a theologic clog,
And yet a strong, instinctive discontent
   Pervades creation ; the domestic dog
Would chuckle at the picture we present,
   Were he as gifted as the human hog,
Whose bacon keeps a god-like essence pent,
   To wallow through a treacherous verdant bog,
Where one, to rise above his struggling brothers,
Must build a firm foundation from the others.

Life is as time and circumstance may choose,
   Not altogether as the man may toil ;
Thus may a fool be able to illuse
   A wiser man who labors in the soil
But who again, by having naught to lose,
   Can bear with easy grace this mortal coil,
While they whose fortunes are the more profuse,
   Inherited or fruit of legal spoil,
Tho' proud of all these valuable talents,
Are thereby hampered.   Nature hits the balance.

He who toils to share the common booty
   Has little time to exercise his wit,
The steady friction of diurnal duty
   Is apt to dull the keener edge of it ;
But, daily labor over, if it suit, he
   May breathe in scented air ; he may sit
Amid some scene replete with solemn beauty
   Where shadows dim mysteriously flit
Among the plumy trees of sable hue,
Whose big blurred hands are gathering the dew.

Where darting, fiery atoms flash and fade,
   While glow-worms burn a tiny emerald light,
Who forage clear of hidden ambuscade
   And vanish at the least alarm from sight ;
Here crickets wheedle shrilly serenade.
   And phosphorent fungus, gleaming sickly white,
Has warned me of a stump along the glade,
   As frequently I stumbled through the night
To Honeywells, from halfway up the mountain,
Which lies about a mile beyond the fountain,

5

To where old Brown, upon the village green,
  Inhabited a cosey little cot—
A better fellow never yet was seen,
  Or more contented with his humble lot.
Many of my leisure hours have been
  Spent by his fire, or 'neath his porch, o'ershot
With climbing foliage, whose tender green
  Lent privacy and beauty to the spot;
Where as we sate my host would oft retail
The floating legends of his native vale,

Or, bringing out a polished ebon flute,
  Send rippling trills of music through the dark.
The echo of the whip-poor-will grew mute,
  The village mongrels even ceased to bark.
His music far and near was in repute,
  And surely he had the vital spark
Of genius, which fires the golden brute,
  Whose grin is fame, whose caprice makes the
      mark
Distinguishing the slave who can create
From he who toils contented with his fate.

When wintry winds blew keen, or chilly drizzle
  Roared drearily around, or drowsy dript,
And seasoned logs sent up a cheery sizzle,
  While scalding tears in the ashes slipt,
The fitful blaze converting silver grizzle
  To silver gilt, as cosily we sipt
A bowl of an exhilarating swizzle,

Compounded from a favorite prescript,
A potion which could ne'er improve our walking,
But added ease and fluency to talking,

We often talked till late into the night,
    I questioning, he giving explanation
With great good humor, often throwing light
    On some lost link or doubtful situation
Which in the tale hereafter written might
    Be some small aid to recognize location,
Or act interpreter to wrong or right,
    Not always free from some equivocation.
I fain would be punctiliously true
In this my tale of Olane and Hoodoo.

Her name was Olane Merley.   Long ago
    She made the poetry of this rhymic tale.
Hoodoo, a queer title, that is so.
    My hero had no other name.   I fail
To follow up his pedigree.   You know
    Him simply as a hunter of the dale
And mountain-side.   So, starting thence, I go
    Cautiously to follow up their trail,
And whether the result be ore or sludge
Time will elucidate, for I'm no judge.

PART I.

Away beyond where rude Atlantic weather
    Beats restlessly along Columbia's shore,
Two lofty hills may yet be seen together,
    Joined by a ridge profusely wooded o'er,

Which, rising greenly through the bracing ether,
    Shelters a verdant valley, sloping lower
To level meadows, gay with flowery bells,
Where sleeps a village known as Honeywells.

No one was e'er reputed to discover
    Beneath or on the land a well of honey,
Unless it may have been some rustic lover
    At tricks most properly defined as funny.
Tradition said the rocks and hills above her
    Somewhere contained a hidden store of money.
But whether buried in a well or cave
Was just the doubtful point nobody gave.

Fact was they had no wells; a mountain stream
    Supplied them water crystallinely pure,
Which, given brains to advertise the scheme,
    Had coined money as a water-cure;
But no, it sparkled downward like a dream,
    A homely blessing, innocent of lure,
From whence the veriest tramp might freely take
E're dancing on to Yellow Lily Lake.

Over a fall, its waters foamy tossed,
    Where spongy mosses wept a trickling rill,
There jewels scattered, disregarding cost,
    With roaring splash or devastating spill,
Then here among the lilies it was lost,
    But iridescent bubbles, floating still,
And glistening foam, in witness of the shock,
Went floating round the base of Castle Rock.

Huge gray old rocks, by wind and weather worn,
   Adorned with colored moss, in queer fret,
With ragged turrets rising up forlorn,
   Stern and silent with a lone regret ;
Half way down, a shelf, where caverns yawn
   Like ruined windows, unexplored yet ;
The rock o'erhanging bars the upper face,
And waters deeply gather round the base.

The lake grows narrow, running by the valley,
   But broadens widely out towards the west,
Skirting the western hill diagonally,
   Water-lilies floating on her breast,
Whose gorgeous single yellow blossoms tally
   To an odd title happily express'd.
'Twas fringed about with graceful trees and bushes,
With here and there a patch of big bulrushes.

A patriarchal tree grows outward o'er
   The lake, about where land and water meet
With Castle Rock ; its trunk appears to bore
   The solid limestone, fitting very neat
Into a rift ; though hollow to the core
   And half decayed, the storm may madly beat
Or work destruction on the higher ground,
That tree is safe, if not so very sound.

For 'tis a monstrous, gnarly, natural freak,
   The bloated, knotty roots set close and stout,
As some enormous pudding-bag might leak
   And harden to the angles spread about,

Or lapping from the edges like a beak
　　To gripe the seamy limestone in and out.
The natives knew the place as Elfin Bower,
And judged it shapen by some mystic power.

Pigeons dwelt among the leafy boughs,
　　Where creepers densely clustered up aloft,
And echo, answering their loving vows,
　　Weirdly multiplied their cooing soft
To most peculiar rolling, rumbling rows,
　　Which, carried by the breeze o'er lake or croft,
Like demon chatter in a tongue satanic,
Suggested half a superstitious panic.

Two ponderous arms like trees of goodly size
　　Went up and outward to a fair height;
Two other mighty limbs went slantingwise
　　Down to the bank, where, chancing to alight
On rich black mould, unable to arise,
　　Had evidently rooted firm and tight;
The branches trailing out upon the water
Had formed a bower fit for Neptune's daughter.

Big vines like serpents twined up from the bank,
　　And clung with spiral fold from limb to limb,
Around the fork the foliage hung rank,
　　And loosely matted by some queer whim
Of Nature o'er a hole.　I had to thank
　　A large oppossum and a quiet swim
(I only caught a transitory view)
For what became a valuable clew.

For, stepping up on lacing vines, I found
   A natural stairway leading to the fork,
Not to be gained directly from the ground.
   The limbs were steep, and slippery to walk;
But from the lake, or by an active bound,
   The wiry vines were gained, from thence to stalk
Along was easy, as I said before,
And by the scars had been in use of yore.

Reaching the fork, I held the vines aside,
   But no opossum there met my view;
A gloomy aperture opened wide,
   Into the trunk.   I did not venture through;
The place was dark.   Perhaps if I had tried
   I might have got into a pretty stew,
While walking, naked, down that yawning gulf,
Opossums bite as savage as a wolf.

A little arbor lay behind the screen,
   From whence I had a comprehensive view.
By peeping through a crack the lake was seen,
   The village opposite by peering through
A knot-hole which had evidently been
   Enlarged in times remote—with care, too—
And on the other side, in front some distance,
A splendid mansion once had known existence.

But now it was a picturesque old ruin.
   Its crumbling relics, delicately stained,
Were carven windows, where the breezes blew in—
   'Twas five and forty years since they were
      paned—

A creeper-covered wall, where sparrows flew in
    And found a shelter every time it rained.
The place is oddly nicknamed Merley's Pyre,
From one who perished over there by fire.

The place was burned completely to the earth,
    Old plate and bronzes lost beyond recall,
Rare tapestries, of almost priceless worth,
    Which hung about the broad and lofty hall,
Old furniture whose carving challenged mirth
    Or merited applause, the fire destroying all,
With costly pictures brought across the seas
From Italy, the land of dirt and fleas,

Where nevertheless are lived illustrious lives,
    There marble grows to something nearly life,
Where music in the atmosphere strives
    To find melodious vent ; a jibbering strife
Of greed and fiery blood and ready knives.
    The lower classes juggle with a knife,
And truly 'tis a pretty tool to summon
A soul to judgment, often through a woman.

The woman is a fateful circumstance
    For good or evil in the universe,
To mesmerize poor mortals with her glance,
    Who laugh, weep, pray, or impotently curse,
While on occasion man, by evil chance,
    Destroys her fragile soul by grief, or worse—
The theme has an unlimited expansion—
A woman fired that same old ruined mansion.

How that occurred will presently transpire,
  As I continue in this narrative,
Which now concerns the honorable squire,
  Or otherwise, as needfully reparative,
Whose gore was very blue, by dam and sire—
  The hue of Reckitt's blue was pale comparative—
A wooden-headed, arrogant old Briton,
Who wanted half the universe to sit on.

A great-grandfather some time in his day
  Had done a deed of service to the nation,
Which, being grateful, granted, by the way,
  Estates, which fell by legal operation
To Merley, who had failed to make them pay
  The larger dividend of speculation.
He therefore emigrated, dealt in stocks,
And built the mansion facing Castle Rocks.

Seen from the balcony the view was fair.
  The wooded mountain, brooding o'er the lake,
Which glittered silvern in the sunny glare,
  And shallow reedy tarn or ferny brake
Where bobs the jerky water-fowl, aware
  For prowling stoat or gliding water-snake;
The black-snake or the copperhead prefers
The higher land, where an odd rattler whirrs.

A shady drive went outward to the road,
  Where towering pine and graceful silver birch
Join spreading beech, now speckled with a load
  Of prickly husks. Here tiny warblers perch,

Immense gray squirrels leap, the bright-eyed toad
   Below expectant waits, with eager lurch,
For variegated lunch, serenely made
From butterfly or moth allured by the shade.

Fresh laden with accumulated sweets,
   Sipped from the cup of weedy flower or plant
That blooms about the place in vivid sheets
   Of brilliant hue, and odors which enchant
The brain with fragrance, here are rustic seats,
   Where Merley eyed his daughter half askance,
For she shone like a gem upon the earth,
He like a rock, so jewels have their birth.

'Tis foolish now to rave about her hair,
   Report says raven, wondrous thick and long ;
Her eyes were dark, perhaps of beauty rare,
   Her figure being perfect, she was strong,
Her face divine—but hang it, who will care
   To hear the hackneyed rigmarole ?—her tongue
I won't disturb, the brain is apt to soften
When female tongues are stirred, I've noticed
     often.

She and her father wandered here together,
   Her rosy, laughing face so fresh and pure,
His features wrinkled like morocco leather,
   With beady eyes, which ragged brows obscure,
A scrubby beard and pimples—know not whether
   They were his birthmark, Nature's signature,
To mark the artificial upper crust,
From healthy brutes, who live much as they must ;

A short, thick neck, a cranium rather shiny,
　　Of figure squat—if this description passes,
His manners surely would, tho' somewhat spiny
　　And supercilious to the lower classes;
Hands and feet unusually tiny,
　　A circumstance admired by the masses
(The eyes of cavern fishes in Kentucky
Grew out of sight from idleness unlucky).

His stony calm had once been rudely shaken
　　By some poor farmer's daughter he had sighted,
And hotly chased, to find himself mistaken;
　　The girl was not disgusted or delighted.
He had to marry her or be forsaken.
　　She wedded him, parentally incited,
And in a year my heroine was born,
The mother dead, and Merley left forlorn.

Intensely selfish, still he had a heart,
　　Or nervous organ, sensitive to grief;
Misfortune smote him like a poisoned dart
　　Cast by the hand of some vindictive thief,
But time rolled on and healed the keener smart,
　　And other cares brought him some relief;
For Olane grew more winsome day by day,
And stole her father's hard old heart away.

For her he sold the old ancestral home,
　　Impoverished by profligate possession;
No need to scan the silly epitome
　　Of what is not remarkable transgression.

He emigrated, satisfied to roam,
   Took an active part in the procession,
And now success had crowned each daring scheme,
Olane nineteen, and fairer than a dream.

He built a factory as times improved
   Some miles away from where he reigned as host,
But kept it quiet, as dignity behooved,
   His ancestry once more became a boast;
The firm was called a company, but proved,
   When Merley later on gave up the ghost,
To be that individual alone,
Whose guiding hand was hitherto unknown.

He was not loved by those he lived among,
   His business methods clipped a little short;
The factory hands declared he should have hung
    For keeping stores where goods were dearly
      bought,
The price deducted from the hardly wrung
   Yet scanty pay, inadequate support
If promptly paid, which rarely occurred,
Yet until then complaints were rarely heard.

'Twas easy trade, the dupes would oft forget
   The tardy pay-day, balanced to the tittle;
When many a man was proved to be in debt,
   The firm would trust those employees a little;
With such as bought elsewhere, at odd times met,
   Their patience was proverbially brittle.
Such promptly were dismissed, on some pretext,
The game to be continued on the next.

But Merley's purse was full, Olane was fair,
    Wealth and beauty, tempting bait for gallants,
She had the choice of such as wandered there,
    But always deemed them wanting in the balance;
Which suited our old hero to a hair,
    Who sent to England for his nephew Clarence,
His brother's son, a dandified what is it,
To pay his wealthy relatives a visit.

" And if," thought Merley, " it should be a match,
    My name would be perpetuated by it,
The property entailed."   Ideas hatch
    Much as an egg contains the proper diet
Whereon the chick evolves.   With great despatch
    An answer came; they chose to gratify it.
The nephew shortly sailed from London city,
Humming the chorus of a comic ditty.

He tragically hummed the vulgar chorus—
    Poor fellow, he was leaving home forever;
The parents bade adieu with grief decorous,
    He'd nearly ruined by a long endeavor.
How many of us know what lies before us?
    When safe across, no lapse of time could sever
The stirring memories of deep emotion
Caused by this trip across the briny ocean.

He brought a pair of pistols, richly mounted,
    For safety in the land of lawless passion—
Such at that time Columbia was accounted;
    His garments were, however, in the fashion.

Then, all the perils of the trip surmounted,
    Excepting the disposal of his ration,
He landed, glorious with Old World knowledge,
Expensively acquired, some at college.

He reached the mansion when a sunset fine
    Had dyed the landscape like a fairy scene;
With gold and crimson sheen the waters shine,
    Amid a tracery of branching green,
Beneath an arch of clustering woodbine,
    The skies, where rose and violet clouds careen,
Presented such a brilliant panorama,
Our noble immigrant ejaculated " Mamma ! "

It was the proper slang among his set
    To thus express a sudden admiration,
But when the fair Olane her cousin met,
    It somehow would not fit the situation.
What it was he stammered, I forget;
    But there he yielded to the fascination
She had for everyone, became her slave,
And fed his hopes on every smile she gave.

His uncle bade him welcome to the place,
    Courteously spoke of their relations,
But noting the expression of his face,
    While Olane lingered, hurried explanations,
And bluntly stated, when alone, the case,
    Finding a ready ear to his persuasions.
Of Olane's inclination naught was said,
But theirs were settled ere they went to bed.

A dinner in elaborate array,
  Attended by a dozen guests or more,
Who chattered in the ordinary way,
  Or gossiped of the sinner who was poor;
They gorged and drenched their fragile earthly
    clay,
  They sipped, or smoked, or listened to a bore,
Then severally drifted off to slumber,
And nightmare visited the greater number.

PART SECOND.

CLARENCE dreamed that his spirit upward soared,
While melodies arose that the earth can ne'er af-
    ford;
Olane had a cold, so she simply lay and snored
  Till the world was up and doing.
Poor fellow, afterwards he miserably fared,
For he haunted her with a fond heart bared
Till the poor young thing grew positively scared
  At such persistent wooing.

'Twas a time of emotion, of the dainty scented
    note,
Of a critical analysis of poetry he wrote,
Of a tinkling guitar in a damp duck-boat
  To a voice in the moonlight thrumming;
Till the stars peered down in amazement sheer,
They bobbed and twinkled in the water clear,
And the fresh-water mermaids wailed "O dear!
  What a wretched mortal strumming!"

At length they had to stuff their little tender finger-
    tips
In the delicate ears, like the shells of lemon-pips,
And their tiny harps floated up like water-lily slips,
    As he bellowed of a beautiful " Bedouin."
In the hammock on the balcony with idle grace
Reclining she listened, as the night fell o'er the
    place,
And a piquant smile crept sweetly o'er her face,
    As she musically murmured " Bruin ! "

'Twas seen as he slept in the sad face dreaming,
It glittered wild in the dark eyes gleaming,
Cupid wrote a wrinkle on his forehead, deeming
    Another affair gone wrong ;
For it mattered nothing to the maiden fair,
Little did she know, and less did she care,
But the zephyrs frolicked in her raven hair,
    As she tripped right merrily along.

So she left him alone to a fancy vain,
And the aimless ache of an empty pain,
To a dark despair, but to worship her again ;
    'Twas a most instructive schooling.
Moping alone, he would moodily sit,
With a glowering jealousy or morbid fit ;
'Twas a curious case of a biter badly bit
    By a Providential ruling.

Morosely he eyed that fair young creature
With lovelorn look, as if to beseech her
To learn of love, to allow him to teach her, `
    With the guile of an ardent tongue ;

Then a merry glance or a conversation
With a rival aroused him to indignation,
And it seemed, by the force of infatuation,
  That the whole wide world went wrong.

For he had no chance. She knew not how to dance,
Old Merley eyed such phenomena askance,
Knowing by experience the force of circumstance
  And the perils of sensation ;
For the simple maid who dances may at first a
      mere scholar be,
Comparatively ignorant of human physiology,
But surely gains a knowledge of a dangerous biol-
      ogy,
  Hence Merley's strong disapprobation.

Clarence ne'er proposed to her, his courage sank,
For he judged he would surely be refused point-
      blank,
And his nature never having been remarkably
      frank
  He naturally took to scheming ;
For her fair young face he could nevermore forget,
He found her power more powerful yet,
As a fish when snared in the fatal net
  Is past all self-redeeming.

I leave him there to get along uneasily enough
In a romance the poetry of which was rather rough,
Tho' probably the trial polished down a cruder
      stuff
  By a process of refining ;
  6

It roused his ambition for a worthier mark,
Tho' his aim was crooked and his course lay dark,
And the life of another hare-brained young spark
   Was one of sore repining.

Olane lived on, unmoved, perhaps, except
That new ideas into subtle being leapt
And faculties awoke which before had slept
   By some magnetic evolution ;
For a sincere love has a power to sway
The fate of another in some occult way,
As an idea works until, lo ! one day
   A people rises up in revolution.

In the tangled web of the wild surmise
That vegetates on what may be hidden from the
      eyes,
For a pure young soul some peril lies,
   Owing to her curious constitution ;
But how that problem was ultimately solved,
And to what extent she became involved,
In proper rotation will be probably resolved
   In the course of the following effusion.

PART THIRD.

How calm and smoothly whirl the wheels of time,
   When the tired laborer returns to rest,
And lays aside his worries with his grime,
   Leaving abstract existence at its best!
A quiet country life contains the prime
   Of happiness to him who has a zest

For tranquil peace and knowledge how to chime
   His life to this ideal; he is blest
With true philosophy.   Down in the village
They theorize on scandal or on tillage.

Down there the moon is shining overhead,
   The sky is clear, stars are twinkling fine,
The simple maid has sought her lowly bed,
   And lights in cottage windows cease to shine,
Tho' an odd swain by blushing beauty led
   Is tramping round untired, a fatal sign
That two more lunatics will shortly wed
   Their love and poverty, a poor combine;
The usual result, a hungry brood
And everlasting scramble after food.

Show me a man bewitched by maiden fair,
   Fallen 'neath the magic of a glance,
Tangled in that enervating snare
   Till matrimony seems his only chance;
Fain would I whisper to that man, " Beware,
   Trust not the cruel luck of circumstance;
Count your resources first, then if you dare
   To pay the fiddler's fee, by all means dance;
Perhaps the fun is purely inoffensive,
But to an amateur it looks expensive."

Samson lived to rue the evil hour
   Wherein he fell beneath Delilah's rule;
All records show that superhuman power
   Availeth not a poor unmarried fool,

The wariest of all are trapped in bower,
   Then made subservient as toy or tool ;
And solitude will turn a temper sour,
   Or cause a fiery temperament to cool,
It leaves a tinge of disappointment sore
On spirits that were angelic before.

Hence marriage is the lesser ill to do,
   Though when the time of trial comes along
It may inflict a mental twinge or two ;
   As sharps and flats occurring in a song,
Joy and misery will jangle through
   The music of the matrimonial gong ;
Sickly yelling babies, awful stew.
   Never being there, may be wrong,
I have no inclination leading from it,
Or spare cash to buy the golden grummit.

Not far from Honeywells, those days, there dwelt
   An odd philosopher, who never knew it,
His buckskin garment cut from softened pelt,
   Knowing, as a hunter, how to do it.
I cannot tell you how his name was spelt,
   His father had no tongue, the Indians drew it,
Delighted with the agony he felt,
   Tho' afterwards he gave them cause to rue it ;
He never spoke to the wee child who cried,
But he would smile each time an Indian died.

No one knew the place wherein they slept,
   The crazy hunter and precocious child
Who by some law of Providence had crept
   Out in the woods when savage hands defiled

Their happy home.   No mother's wise precept
   Had trained his mind; he grew up strong and
     wild;
In woodland craft he ranked as an adept,
   Of ignorant virtue, always unbeguiled,
He rarely spoke, excepting when they made
Odd trips to town for purposes of trade.

Skins of various animals they slew,
   Venison or other kinds of meat;
Honey from the hollow trees that grew
   And furnished hives to store the fragrant
     sweet
Patiently hoarded by the wild bees, who
   By flying straightway home invite defeat
Of their united effort; knowing two,
   When loosed apart, will join at their retreat,
The hunter marks and flies them far asunder,
The air-lines crossing o'er the luscious plunder.

Times change.   The Indians migrated west,
   Settlers came, the wilderness was tilled;
The scarred old hunter laid him down to rest,
   His spirit went to join the foemen killed;
The son remained, a mark of interest,
   But public curiosity was chilled
By evil rumors, doubtfully expressed,
   So accident arranged it as he willed;
They shunned not he alone, but where they saw
     him,
Which made it very comfortable for him.

He grew up nameless till a drunken nigger,
  Who listened to the stories that were told
Of cunning trap or an unerring trigger,
  How he would seem to vanish through the
    mould;
He leapt with extraordinary vigor,
  The number of his tricks was manifold,
Yet was he handsome, and of goodly figure,
  Impervious to either heat or cold;
They marked poor Sambo turn a whiter blue,
Who said the boy was certainly Voodou.

" Hoodoo?" repeated they, a slight mistake.
  The darky never noticed it or gave
Much fuller information, save to make
  Them understand that he had been a slave
In Southern States, where, venturing to take
  His liberty, 'twas Voodou's will to save
Him from the bloodhounds tracking through the
    brake.
  That afternoon poor Sambo found a grave
By walking in the lake, wherein he sunk,
His friend escaped, tho' both were very drunk.

His quondam comrade, stupefied with drink,
  Vociferously yelled awhile for aid,
But stood and watched the helpless negro sink,
  The water being far too deep to wade;
Then rushing past and leaping from the brink,
  The hunter's son dived in the lake, and made

A futile search; the undertow, I think,
   Had carried off the body, to be laid
In some obscure mud-hole, nevermore
To see the light.   Then Hoodoo swam ashore.

The garbled tale had left an evil fame
   Like a dark cloud about his curly head,
Few but who were much inclined to blame
   His evil arts for Sambo's weakly head.
They dubbed him Hoodoo, and he bore the blame,
   The object of a vaguely cherished dread,
Except, maybe, a tender-hearted dame
   Who sorrowed o'er the lonely life he led,
Deeming his talents wasted as a woodman,
Or dreaming he was turned into a goodman.

But Hoodoo lived beneath the forest tree,
   And never yet had fared a whit the worse;
High in the mountain, satisfied to be
   Sole ruler in his little universe;
A wild existence, prone to disagree
   With civilized ideas, his perverse
Philosophy preferring to be free;
   He scorned the civil system as a curse,
Whereby the mob are pitilessly set
To slave, without the breeding cattle get.

Over the hills a shallow valley forms,
   A lovely place, of verdant mossy slope
And hollow stump, wherein the wild bee swarms,
   Where creepers ramble, hanging down like rope

From hoary trees, fit bulwark from the storms
   Of either side; a view of ample scope
Toward the southern sky, whose sunlight warms;
   Here deer feed, the timid rabbit lopes,
And chipmunks glide amid the curling frond
Of graceful fern or gnarly roots beyond.

Where flowers in rainbow guise are gayly peep-
     ing,
   And rhododendron cast a sober shade,
Wiry vines are sinuously creeping
   Amid the wreck their harlot habits made,
Sparkling insects, tiny spangles leaping,
   Dodge the odd humming-birds which haunt the
     glade,
Their slender bills in nectar whilom steeping,
   Like scraps of fire from a sunset strayed,
And butterflies go wavering about,
Lost in delicious paroxysms of doubt.

Where rivulets diffuse a diamond tear,
   Or gurgle down a miniature glen,
From dizzy little cliffs intoning clear,
   And whirling in some wee aquatic den,
Where hungry microscopic horrors leer,
   Or dart around in crazy fury, then,
Demurely gliding, ends a short career
   Lost in the bowels of a pigmy fen,
Bloated reeds and juicy-looking grass,
Nodding and flirting over the morass.

Here Hoodoo lived away from everyone.
    His hut lay in a lofty, sheltered nook
From here to hunt the woods, or sagely con
    The lessons in Creation's open book,
More varied vanities than Babylon
    Displayed on earth, in air, or rhyming brook ;
All practised earnestly, the poetry gone
    For philosophic eyes, which keenly look ;
Every separate item in the list
Cancelling some other to exist.

He viewed a thousand tragedies a week,
    In every tone of this uncanny key ;
He noted how the strong absorbed the weak,
    Unless they had the policy to flee ;
Each queer device or variegated freak
    A veil to hide a sudden treachery ;
Rejoicing that he was not doomed to sneak
    Along the social gutter furtively,
As many honest men must do to live,
Where good men work and philanthropic give.

'Twas natural to hunt his daily meat.
    Exciting to be hunted by the bear,
Whose massive hams are very good to eat ;
    He knew the dens they fancied as a lair,
Their skins were valuable, cured neat.
    He hunted bees when he had time to spare,
And fished the little river at his feet ;
    The only outlet of the lake ran there,
An easy road to travel, for he knew
The way to build the Indian canoe.

In summer-time, when skies were burning blue,
    This woodland life was very nice indeed.
Game to furnish food and pastime too,
    Furs to deck a springy couch of reed,
No fetid drudgery to worry through,
    Unbound by any social law or creed,
His log-built hut a shelter from the dew
    And storeroom for future time of need ;
For winter came this way, with snow and ice,
When life up here was not so very nice.

When vegetation droops in damp decay,
    Root and branch in paralytic doze,
Tempests gurgle round in frosty play,
    Hurling rainy sleet or pelting snows,
Those dead old chumps a slimy face display,
    From dripping tear, or rivulet which flows
Down on the thorny skeletons that sway,
    Weeping for bygone joy and present woes ;
But spring returns and soothes away the pain,
And summer paints creation up again.

Oft when a roebuck fell before his gun
    He stript the hide, and hung it up to bleach,
Then loading his canoe with venison,
    He paddled to a town in easy reach,
Selling it, and with the money won
    Procuring ammunition, filling each
Necessity he knew; at setting sun
    Returning down the lake, along the beach,
And crossing over from the northern shore
Entered the river, reaching home once more.

Olane had often seen him thus returning,
  And naturally was a little curious,
Betraying sudden eagerness for learning
  To navigate.   Her father, not penurious
On points whereon her august will was turning,
  Bought her a skiff, of style somewhat luxurious,
To gratify her *bona-fide* yearning ;
  'Twas very genuine, this sudden notion,
  And she betrayed some gratified emotion.

Oft, in the course of ordinary chat,
  Olane had heard about the hermit youth,
Had even passed him, when she noticed that
  Report for once had partly spoken truth,
For he was handsome, active as a cat.
  Tho' evil rumor, with a venomed tooth,
Had poisoned his fair fame, the tale fell flat
  On Olane's ear, she heeded not, forsooth.
He followed her with an admiring glance,
But neither spoke, until they found a chance.

When, after many a slip and nervous shiver,
  The dainty plaything moved at her command,
One day she entered the forbidden river,
  Which led between the hill and forest land,
Excitement sending a delightful quiver
  Through every nerve, when, drawn up on the
      sand,
She spied a bark canoe, enough to give her
  The missing clue ; so landing near at hand,
Where all around the rushes rose above her,
She sallied forth, determined to discover.

Then Hoodoo gained the bottom of the hill
    Through flowery jungle, tangle truly wiry,
And each, astonished, paused to gaze their fill
    Or make an entry in a mental diary,
While vague, sweet music seemed to mutely
      thrill
    Along a glance of mutual inquiry ;
Then Olane turned, whereby a wayward frill
    Hooked fast among the vegetation briary,
Utterly upset the maiden's gravity,
And stuck like an inherited depravity.

I might have said the centre of, but then
    The metre called for something not so long,
Also 'tis doubtful if my erring pen
    Has stated the idea so very wrong,
When damsels gaze on very handsome men,
    With sparkling eyes, of shapely limb and
      strong,
Who set a person on their feet again,
    Without a single movement of the tongue.
This Hoodoo did, most courteously grave,
For courtesy is common to the brave.

She fell, of course, with that peculiar grace
    The blunders of the fairer sex announce,
Nor rolled, as any man would, and debase
    The language by a word I can't pronounce ;
And then, her feet regained, with blushing face,
    While Hoodoo frees her dress, her tact sur-
      mounts

An awkward pause by asking if the place
　　Was equal to the wonderful accounts
Which rumor gave, or if tradition lied.
Then Hoodoo volunteered to be her guide.

'Twas wrong.　Perhaps this was the time to leave,
　　But Olane was not open to distrust,
Besides, a pistol lay inside her sleeve,
　　With which her aim was usually just.
No reason had he given her to grieve,
　　So, having broken through the outer crust
Of their reserve, determined to achieve
　　The feat, she meekly followed in the dust
Along the bank, till, parting through a screen
Of hanging vines, a beaten path was seen.

But Hoodoo, ere they started, had required
　　A promise from Olane to never speak
Of what she saw, as it was not desired
　　That all should know the secret of the creek ;
Her curious nature thus unduly fired,
　　With palpitating heart and flaming cheek,
She pierced the thorny belt to this retired
　　Retreat where Hoodoo dwelt, and one might seek
Another way in vain ; a precipice
Bounded in every other side but this.

And much she saw which served to animate her.
　　They scaled the highest peak, not pointed, but
A little hollowed, like an ancient crater,
　　While bushes round the rim completely shut

All view out from the distant speculator;
  Here was built his humble little hut.
From this high point, unseen, the fair spectator
  Could view the hamlet, by a shorter cut.
And one more circumstance to fascinate her,
  From here her father's mansion could be seen,
  Encircled in a ring of living green.

Then Hoodoo made a fire, prepared a meal,
  The fuel charcoal; as he spread the feast,
Inviting her, with hospitable zeal,
  To share therein, as might some rustic priest
Offer a sacrament to those who kneel.
  And she, from all formality released,
Humored her host, but talked and laughed a deal
  More than she ate or drank, but never ceased
To question Hoodoo of his life and history,
Which hitherto was enveloped in mystery.

He answered her. He could not recollect
  The outline of a mother's kindly face;
His early home by fire and savage wreck'd,
  The mother perished. In his father's case,
They tortured him—no white man need expect
  A scrap of mercy from the Indian race;
His tongue cut out, they left him to collect
  Sufficient strength to roast—escape, and chase.
How Hoodoo got away he never knew.
Then showed her Indian scalp-locks—forty-two.

They settled ere the turnpike was a track.
  Then pointed out his tomb, a heap of stone.

His father lived till thirteen years back,
  But more of his life was never known,
Or of the Indians' murderous attack,
  Except his father's trophies.   All alone
Here Hoodoo lived, nor ever suffered lack
  Of aught till now.   The meditative tone
And quaint remark conveyed a certain charm
For she who questioned him without alarm.

So when they parted on the river shore
  She told him that she meant to come again,
And wistfully poor Hoodoo lingered o'er
  The slender fingers of the fair Olane,
Who promised to display, the night before,
  A lamplight, through a crimson window-pane,
At ten o'clock precisely, nothing more,
  And she would come, unless it chanced to rain.
So Hoodoo always sat upon the rock
And watched the house till after ten o'clock.

And nearly every day they came together,
  Why it happened so I cannot say ;
His manly heart had never known a tether,
  Her curiosity was hard to sway ;
Trifles lighter than a downy feather,
  Accumulating fast, may block the way.
Since first they met they loved, regardless whether
  It led to stormy sea or sheltered bay
Of wedded life, not shorn of all its rancor,
For vessels labor, even when at anchor.

This being so, 'tis useless to describe
    The oral outbreak of the mesmeric spasm,
Experience proving such a diatribe
    To be a sort of moral cataplasm,
Opening pores to the chilling jibe,
    Or drawing forth a festering sarcasm
From some among that deedless, caustic tribe
    Ever seeking out a vacant chasm
Wherein to shed their natural impediment,
Of minds diseased, an acrid, odious sediment.

Her father saw the roses on her cheek,
    Noted her lengthy absence every day;
Enormous lunches taken seemed to speak
    Of sharpened appetite or picnic gay.
Her pleasure-boat would vanish like a streak;
    He never wondered where she went astray,
Deeming it a momentary freak,
    Whose cost he was contented to defray.
Their courtship prospered finely, no censorious
Or meddling tongue to mar a romance glorious.

Romantic souls, I envy their beatitude,
    Their fervent love, and mutual admiration,
For now their drifting souls assumed an attitude
    Defiant to the law of social station.
Proverbially deaf to warning platitude,
    No woman could resist the combination;
They quickly lost their longitude and latitude
    In seas of sentiment and palpitation,

And, caring little whither they were carried,
They sneaked away one morning and were mar-
    ried.

They went by different ways, she in her boat
    Along the shore, to the nearest town ;
His bark canoe that day contained the coat
    Worn by his father once—'twas worn and brown,
But hid the leather suit, which might denote
    A hurried flight ; her shabby veil half down,
Her dress was poor ; the parson seemed to dote,
    He only saw a country girl and clown ;
And as the bridegroom had no name to tell,
He signed the book as Hoodoo Honeywell.

She hurried swiftly home, the wedding-ring
    And marriage document safe out of sight ;
Her walk had not the same elastic spring,
    She said she felt a little tired to-night.
Her father never noticed anything,
    Excepting that her eyes were very bright,
And when her cousin, asking her to sing,
    She graciously complied, he thought, " All
        right ! "
Then lights were lit, and Olane went to bed,
Where Hoodoo marked a tiny spark of red.

The honeymoon was probably delicious,
    That people may imagine for themselves,
Too close acquaintanceship is injudicious ;
    I leave their early pairing to the elves

7

To tattle of, for I am not malicious,
    Or one who systematically delves
In sacred soil; such conduct is pernicious,
    To maiden meditation on the shelves;
But that they had a happy time I know,
She always went there fast and came back slow.

Human logic cannot analyze
    The gas of Love, or limn the mystic twinkle
In lovelit eye, or fitly eulogize
    Osculent ventures on the rosebud crinkle,
Nor may it tamper in a manner wise
    With angel smile, or tone of silver tinkle.
If any man would fain immortalize
    Himself and theme, and teach the world a
        wrinkle,
Love well and wisely, then relate the tale,
And ten to one he'll miserably fail.

Oh, sanguine fools, who would delineate
    The blissful misery of summer rain,
The dreamy flash of tints that scintillate,
    In nearly ripened fields of sunny grain;
The ethereal glint of love or hate
    Which alternates in every lover's brain
Let Cupid settle, for ye meditate,
    And fabricate, and recreate in vain;
Unless the world your rhapsodies may thank
For many a profanely uttered blank.

Some weeks passed by, a time of pure bliss
    And anxious caution for the wedded pair;

For Olane's father lately seemed to miss
   Her presence.   Often he would oddly stare
At her perplexed, as hoping to dismiss
   Unpleasant doubt, and Clarence everywhere ;
But Hoodoo calmed her fears with a kiss,
   Praying his wife to come and live up there.
And so it was agreed, she had consented,
When something happened and she was prevented.

The sun that eventide hung burning low
   On the horizon like a red doubloon
In rainbow waves and changing fitful throe
   Of yellow radiance, which deepening soon
To solemn glory, as the dying glow
   Ruddily dyed the glittering lagoon ;
Then dreamy darkness vaguely blent with woe,
   Moody stars and melancholy moon ;
And Olane, by her chamber-window weeping,
Was under lock and key for safer keeping.

The lamp burnt clearly on the inlaid table,
   Amid the costly foreign bric-à-brac ;
Her mind was running in a perfect Babel,
   Her happiness had gone to sudden wrack ;
Some spy had told her father quite a fable
   Of what was being done behind his back ;
Hoodoo knew of nothing, she unable
   To warn him of the foes upon his track ;
Merley raved, and swore to have the life
Of Hoodoo, who had dared to make her wife.

" Two desperadoes wait," her father said.
    The tears welled up into her lovely eyes,
For Olane, living now in constant dread,
    Was sadly puzzled how to signalize.
'Twas nearly ten; the signal, white or red,
    Meant no or yes; but then Hoodoo was wise.
Green panes were also there, so she sped
    And caused the flame to greenly sink or rise.
Soon Hoodoo saw the color flash and fade,
And, fearing for Olane, became afraid.

Regardless of the danger he incurred
    By trespassing at night within the wall,
He crossed the lake to gain a cheering word,
    And 'neath her window made an owlish call,
When suddenly a loud report was heard,
    While Hoodoo felt the whistle of a ball,
And seeing figures moving up, preferred
    To simulate the wounded by a fall
Among the shrubbery, but wriggled on,
So that when they arrived, the game was gone.

Clarence ran from where he thought he saw him,
    And rushed into the clutches of the stranger,
Who promptly choked the figure coming for him,
    To lessen odds and put him out of danger,
Although poor Clarence feebly strove to claw him
    'Twas underneath the bushes, where a manger
Received the rotten garbage; there to draw him,
    Unconscious from the throttle, took the ranger,
A moment more, and with a farewell thump
He cleared the wall at one terrific jump.

Then, swiftly running to the waterside,
　　Embarked, nor ceased to powerfully urge
Across the moonlit water, but was spied,
　　For two more bullets gritted through the verge
And bow of his canoe, so Hoodoo tried
　　Upsetting it, then managed to emerge
And breathe unseen, when, drifting with the tide
　　To where he heard a pigeon's mournful dirge,
Dived underneath, and came up in the shade
Of Elfin Bower, unhurt and undismayed.

He climbed up in the fork, and felt a rift,
　　The foliage concealing him from harm,
Behind the matted creepers made a shift
　　To crawl therein, and found it nice and warm ;
None could see the place without a gift
　　Of second-sight, and though he felt a qualm,
He had to let events at present drift,
　　While poor Olane, aroused by wild alarm,
Had seen his flight, and being wide awake,
Now deemed him at the bottom of the lake.

Part Four.

　　By the window on the stair,
　　With his old head bare
　　And his scanty silver hair
　　　　Blowing wild,
　　Sat old Merley with a gun,
　　And a face devoid of fun,
　　Like a stark automaton,
　　　　Unreconciled.

His doughty nephew Clarence watched from un-
    derneath a bush,
While a pair of paid detectives waited ready for a
    rush
For a burglar they expected ; 'twas a snare laid to
    crush
        The lover of the old man's child.

        " Hark ! " he muttered, " what was that ?
        A bat, or maybe rat,
        Or the anthem of a cat
            Upon the tiles ! "
        It was Hoodoo softly creeping
            Unto where Olane was sleeping,
        In spite of all their peeping,
            Crafty wiles.
Merley lifted up his gun, and took a rapid aim,
Pulled the trigger with a bang and sudden gush of
    flame,
Then Hoodoo fell, and Merley's face, thus having
    bagged his game,
        Wore a grin like an angry crocodile's.

        Simultaneous with the bang,
        A shriek of terror rang,
        Then a window with a clang
            Opened wide,
        There Olane, with raven tress
        Flowing o'er her snowy dress,
        Wrung her hands in sore distress,
            A widowed bride.

Then a yell of disappointment, when the body was
    not found,
A figure flying o'er the wall at one terrific bound,
A volley, and the deed was done, and Hoodoo
    surely drowned,
      Being wounded—anyway he must have
      died.

      They captured his canoe.
      It was pierced through and through,
      With a stain thereon they knew
        To be blood.
      And Clarence came, his nose
      Battered up by heavy blows,
      Plenty gore upon his clothes,
        And filthy mud.
Merley complimented him for being very brave,
And said the darkness must have been in favor of
    the knave,
'Twas lucky that the burglar had found a ready
    grave,
      Saving funeral expenses, it was good.

      Olane, as I have said,
      Hurried quickly out of bed,
      Her weary soul like lead
        Dully sinking,
      And she saw his rapid flight,
      Through the amber mellow night,
      In an agony of fright,
        Ever thinking

Of a wee canoe upsetting, and the awful, sudden
    doom
Of her wounded hero, drowning in the distant
    gloom,
And the white face gleaming of a dead bride-
    groom,
      With the stars overhead soft blinking.

      Then Clarence and old Merley,
      After all this hurly-burly,
      As the time was getting early,
      Said good-night.
      And either went his way,
      To slumber till the day
      Arose to chase away
      Visions bright.
The old fellow dreamed that his enemy was dead.
To the nephew it seemed that the maid and he were
    wed,
But Olane sadly tossed and tumbled round upon
    the bed
      Till the dawning of the morning light.

      Then the night died away,
      The light of cheery day
      Overpowering the ray
      Of moon or stars,
      And she rose to face the morrow
      With a vein of bitter sorrow,
      For the loss of lover hero
      Keenly jars.

The romance of ideal may possess a stubborn
    glamour,
But a lover warm and real, be it husband or par-
    amour,
When dead, may leave a memory that bruises like
    a hammer,
        To mark a tender soul with deadly scars.

        Why I cannot tell,
        But I know it happened well,
        A queer thing befell
        The clever father,
        For the virgin pangs of gout
        Had begirt his toes about,
        Reporting back, no doubt,
        Like liquid lava.
The cynical young spriglet who assisted at the scene
Came down with swelled proboscis and his optics
    blue and green.
        The staid old doctor said
        They were both to stay in bed,
        And as both were overfed,
        'Twas serious, rather.

        Her father growing worse,
        Being free, she chose to nurse.
        He who put this heavy curse
        Upon her life
        The detectives richly paid
        By the widow they had made,
        In the action of their trade,
        Any strife.

As for Clarence, tho' she knew the part he took in
    this affair,
How he had spied and followed her to Hoodoo's
    rocky lair,
So great was his assurance that he still continued
    there,
      In the hope of gaining her to be his wife.

Part Five.

The first effect of violent exertion
    Is usually seen in the reaction.
Hoodoo felt, tho' wet from his immersion,
      Great satisfaction.

Exhaustive to the system more or less,
    The strain had left his vital forces lower;
Nature rarely fails to show distress
      For wasted store.

So that when Hoodoo felt the crisis past,
    A languor o'er his spirit slowly stealing
Grew until he recognized, at last,
      A hungry feeling.

So taking out a wallet he proceeded
    To fill the aching void with something solid;
Nature gaining what she badly needed,
      His soul grew stolid,

Even revolted at a noble slice
    Of sundried fat because it was not lean,
For satiated hunger has a spice
      Of something mean.

Curling up, he slumbered, warm and cosey,
  Amid the crumbling wood therein collected,
And when the sun shot up a warning rosy,
    His hiding-place inspected.

The trunk was nearly hollow to the bark,
  And slanted gently down into the rock;
The lower part, of course, was very dark,
    But widened with the stock.

Crumbling wood in lieu of sodden timber,
  Flint and steel supplied a spark to scorch;
Breathing fanned it to a glowing cinder
    Wherewith to light a torch.

For ingenuity in compensation
  From rotten wood devised a wick and handle,
The slice of fat, and, lo! illumination,
    A home-made candle.

Like most things made at home, a thing of woe,
  For Benedict to ponder over sadly;
I cannot swear that it is ever so,
    But this was burning badly.

The light enabled Hoodoo's prying eyes
  To pierce the gloom as far as he intended,
When he discovered, much to his surprise,
    The passage was not ended.

A tree that grew to such abnormal girth
  Was surely many hundred years shaping,
And at the lower end into the earth
    A cavity was gaping.

The butt had split and rotted in the rift,
   Leaving a narrow cavern showing there;
The flame also betrayed an inward drift
     Of moving air.

Stepping through, he found a passage trending
   Over to the right, then rising higher,
Stalagmite and sparry gravel blending
     With slushy mire.

Ascending cautiously o'er tangled roots
   That spread along the mould or muddy dripping,
Which now and then would coil about his boots
     And set him tripping,

But passing slowly on, the road grew firmer,
   Percolating water ceased to drop,
Yet echoed with a dull, metallic murmur,
     Or hollow slop.

The place was bored with interlacing tunnel,
   Picturesque with sphere or ragged sliver,
Worn by rush of subterranean runnel
     Of ancient river,

Fossil seaweed, partly buried shell
   From which the softer limestone had abraded,
Bits of coral petrified as well
     The walls brocaded.

Here the roof grew gradually wider;
   White cocoons were hung in many a cranny,
Each attended by a hairy spider
     Ferociously uncanny.

Fissures gleamed with monster crystal teeth,
  Sharply jutting forth at every angle,
Casting back the glimmer from beneath
    In diamond spangle.

Then by and by he blundered on a cave,
  All curious with hanging stalactite,
Which here and there a tiny sparkle gave
    From Hoodoo's light.

The feeble light began to wave and flicker ;
  It shed a ghostly glare round the den
Where once an Indian wizard brewed the liquor
    To physic sick red men.

A certain sense of gloomy superstition
  Clung about him like a sleepy drug,
But logic, with oracular precision,
    Echoed " Humbug ! "

The grime of ages formed an arabesque,
  Patterned over with design fantastic,
With hanging tassel petrified grotesque
    And pennon plastic.

Spiny roof and queerly carven wall,
  With gobelin tapestry incrusted o'er,
And dust lay like a funereal pall
    Along the floor.

A beaten track ran in a winding strip,
  Bordered by a crooked printed figure
Which might have been inflicted by a whip,
    But rather bigger.

A trail whose course the level floor pursuing,
　　Rising as it reached the outer side,
Ending in a fissure choked with ruin
　　　　Of outlet wide.

Through crevices the daylight faintly filtered,
　　And here a vine had shot a weakly spray,
Branching yellowly and nearly wilted
　　　　From lack of sunny ray.

A beaten track, as one might often trundle
　　A bucket from the outer wall and back,
Circling round a shapeless roll or bundle
　　　　Like a sack.

It lay back in a corner of the cave
　　Near a heap of miscellaneous lumber,
Emitting odors matched by nothing save
　　　　A crushed cucumber.

Hoodoo quietly drew away the stuff
　　And made a passage to the outer shelf,
But stayed inside—the prospect was too rough
　　　　To show himself.

Tho' waving fern and clustered vine were growing
　　About the edge, it was a doubtful case—
The ledge on Castle Rock was plainly showing
　　　　From Merley's place.

Then gradually poured a flood of light
　　And bathed the sepulchre in liquid glory,
Dissipating many years of night,
　　　　But not their story.

The dreary sense of peril seemed to go,
   Fading like the odor of a drug,
Logic whispered, " There, I told you so !
     Humbug ! "

In streamed the daylight, falling fair and full
   Across the figure whence the reek exuded,
From where a sadly battered human skull
     Protruded.

The teeth had fallen from the crumbling thing,
   Among the dust which lay in ridgy swirls,
And mingled oddly with a broken string
     Of yellow pearls.

The tiny bones which form the hand or foot,
   Dust-corroded, on the floor rolled,
Hustled here and there in the soot
     Of years untold.

The brittle robe, tho' badly desiccated,
   Clove unto the frame and served to hide it;
Not the slightest tremor indicated
     What lay inside it.

Staff in hand, our pertinacious rover,
   Moved instinctively by vague distrust,
Capsized the skeleton and rolled it over
     Among the dust.

Straightway upreared a horrible bouquet
   Of vibrant flattened heads all scaly shining,
Sparkling eyes and forky tongues at play
     And stalky bodies twining,

Each hissing serpent busy agitating
   The warning music of a horny rattle,
And one enormous fellow meditating
     Immediate battle.

The fragile shelter of their snaky youth
   Upset, no wonder they should execrate him,
Or try and nail him with the hollow tooth,
     To salivate him.

Darting viciously and quickly coiling,
   Rage but rendering them more repulsive,
A pretty queer kettle set a-boiling
     By act impulsive.

His trusty staff went swinging through the air,
   Feet an agile devil's hornpipe dancing,
Perspiration dripping from his hair
     From sudden prancing ;

The consequences of a single miss,
   Making life exceedingly unstable ;
The den of forty thieves compared to this
     A mere fable.

An odd one wriggled out upon the rocks,
   Others bravely sought to hold their own,
But dying by the dint of heavy knocks,
     Soon Hoodoo was alone.

Then curiosity advanced a claim,
   The rush of speculation running rife
On who the dead might be, and what his name
     And bygone life.

The place was dry and finely ventilated;
    Reasons for the rattlers are various;
One often hears of serpents congregated;
        They are gregarious.

A brief examination would suffice
    To grant a key to fit the mystery,
And bare a record of ingenious vice,
        The wizard's history.

On grimy shelves around the gruesome vault
    Lay many a precious relic of the past,
Murderous-looking weapons of assault
        Staring aghast.

Phials of rudely fashioned earthenware,
    In which the doubtful medicine had dried,
Arrow-heads and gems unique and rare,
        Lay side by side.

Wampum from the far Pacific Sea,
    Beaten plates of yellow virgin gold,
Rotten fabrics, priceless once, maybe,
        Lay fold on fold.

Human skulls with long, discolored teeth,
    Mummied snakes and lizards were hob-nobbing,
Which time had decked with many a dusty wreath
        Crazily bobbing.

Idols reached and leered in vacant pomp,
    With limbs misshapen, who appeared to strive
To lure the corpse into some evil romp,
        As when alive.

8

Earthen lamps in every little niche
　　Spoke a somewhat cultivated ease,
From which protruded yet the rusty wick,
　　Now innocent of grease.

A hollowed rock containing leafy mould,
　　Bloated'vases, ancient crockery,
Tomahawks from off the handles rolled,
　　As if in mockery.

Here long ago a mighty wizard dwelt,
　　Who wielded " Humbug " with a steady hand,
Until his potent influence was felt
　　Throughout the land,

From herbs distilling many a subtle draught,
　　Cooling salve or some infernal lotion,
Ere mighty spirits fashioned wings to waft
　　The white wolves o'er the ocean.

Here repaired the Indian canoe,
　　The rugged warrior, or simple maiden,
To hear the oracle of Manitou,
　　With sacrifices laden,

And laid ashore 'neath the tree of terror,
　　Woful chanting, rhythmic supplication,
Many a fearful tale of savage error
　　And solemn invocation.

An earthen vessel full of glowing coke,
　　Moistened moss and spices added to it,
Obscured Castle Rock with odorous smoke
　　Outpouring through it.

Humbug, playing an audacious rôle,
  Imposes on a crude imagination ;
It finds a home in many an honest soul
    Throughout creation.

A wave of chill presentiment goes stealing
  O'er those who view the necromantic vision ;
The aromatic vapor fades, revealing
    The great magician.

Great and small, the mighty or the weak,
  Bow before the fearful apparition
In abject horror, while he deigned to speak
    The mystical decision.

A tube or packet falling in the lake,
  Conveying physic, as he gave instruction,
Of where, or when, and how they were to take,
    Or possible destruction.

They frantically paddle out of sight,
  The rocks resounding with a peal of thunder,—
A copper gong lay handy there to smite,
    He got the plunder,

And maybe got a blessing from a chief
  Whose barren squaw had ta'en a soporific
Beneath the tree, and grown to their relief
    Undoubtedly prolific.

Humbug plays on earth no humble rôle,
  Success arises by its operation ;
Its fountain-head is every greedy soul
    Throughout creation.

Hoodoo, with a much-astonished face,
  Yet hailed the venture as a happy hit;
It answered every purpose of the case,
    In all ways fit—

Rude and rugged to the last degree,
  Solitary as an eagle's nest,
A place wherein the fair Olane and he
    Could safely rest.

The labor of a day eradicated
  The musty wreck of foul dilapidation;
When clean, the cave already indicated
    An air of habitation.

He cut a clearing in the vines and fern
  Around the fissure, which afforded light;
Yet prying eyes that way might safely turn—
    'Twas out of sight.

The hollowed rock, when full of springy reed
  And spread with fleecy furs, made up a bed,
Arms lay on a ledge, in case of need,
    Near by the head.

For late that night he swam around the bluff,
  And with a spare canoe, concealed before,
Had brought a miscellaneous lot of stuff
    Safely ashore,

And, lowering a rope from off the fork,
  Had hauled it up and carried to the grotto
With silent speed, for action, rarely talk,
    Was Hoodoo's motto.

Finding many ornaments intact,
  He decorated as his fancy ran ;
Next evening found the grot, in point of fact,
    Quite spick and span.

A mat of bark kept in the mellow beams,
  Lent by earthen lamps secured aloft,
Backward cast by scintillating gleams,
    Or sparkle soft.

Ancient battle-axes hung around,
  Curious vases stood about the floor,
Arrow-heads and knives of flint were found
    By the score.

The idols still retained their former pride,
  But that he venerated does not follow ;
He kept his father's cherished scalps inside,
    They being hollow.

And every time the outlaw entered here
  'Twas like the advent of a jolly gnome ;
Every shadow seemed to disappear,
    For it was home.

The idols seemed to wear a friendly grin,
  And tried to swell with silent inward laughter,
As if to murmur, " Lots of fun, come in,
    And more after."

E'en the venerable sculptured owl
  Winked a carven eye in stony joy,
And strove to hoot, with an approving scowl,
    " Good boy ! "

A battered skull pathetically flung
   A hollow smile of welcome from its lair,
Inferring silently, " I once was young.
     Ah, I've been there ! "

Not these alone, but everything beside
   Appeared to wear a jovial expression—
Perhaps a fancy, nurtured by the pride
     Of full possession—

And when 'twas dinner-time, or winds were chill,
   A crock of burning charcoal in the room,
Wedged into a crevice of the hill,
     Which carried off the fume.

Many a juicy steak was here prepared.
   The vapor had a value, too, as well ;
Once or twice a clown was badly scared
     By an odd smell,

And wildly fled, for fear some evil ghoul
   Had raised this tempting odor as a lure
To draw a Christian soul to orgies foul—
     Infernal overture—

So that a woodland walk which used to run
   O'er Castle Rock at once became deserted ;
There goblins gathered, darksome deeds were done,
     It was asserted.

A ghastly legend circulated round
   Of ghostly figures who at midnight sauntered—
An ebon shade with Hoodoo, lately drowned ;
     The place was haunted.

So here he might have lived and later died,
  As did the former tenant long before him,
A victim unto Merley's iron pride,
    Had fate passed o'er him.

Who lives that can avoid those unseen hands
  Which shape the destinies of every age?
How they dealt with Merley now demands
    Another page.

PART SIXTH.

Returning to the mansion where old Merley lay in
    pain,
We find him well attended by his daughter, fair
    Olane,
Who, sad and paler than her wont, yet scorning to
    complain,
  Mechanically moved about the place.
Not a syllable escaped her lip anent the brutal
    plan
By which the cold conspirators had slain a better
    man ;
But her eyes were losing lustre and her cheek was
    growing wan,
  And they daily marked a change upon her
    face ;
At night, when she retired, she would sit and sadly
    scan
  The waters where the tragedy took place.

One starlight night, a fortnight after Merley laid
    the trap,
She was seated at the casement in a sombre-colored
    wrap,
When she heard a little gravel on the window
    faintly tap,
  Like the signal of a sly associate;
And opening the casement, in the garden down be-
    low
She beheld a dusky outline which she somehow
    seemed to know;
But a heavy step approaching, as if fearing it a foe
  She dimly saw the form evaporate,
But heard a stealthy footfall on the arbor portico,
  Where the starry twinkle did not penetrate.

Then Clarence turned the corner—Olane knew him
    in the dark,
His identity established by a tiny moving spark
From a big cigar he usually carried, as a mark
  Of extravagantly cultivated ease—
Who, pausing opposite, assumed a sentimental
    pose,
Then murmured half aloud, "She sleeps! Incom-
    parable rose,
Would that I were thy stalk!" and blew his
    lacerated nose,
  Which continued most unpleasantly obese,
Also unpoetic. So relapsing into prose
  He muttered, "And no other legatees."

Then, sighing, went along the walk, resuming his
    cigar,
Sat down upon the arbor-step, producing a
    guitar,
And was tuning up the instrument with unmelodi-
    ous jar,
    When he found his choice regalia was out;
He therefore struck a lucifer, which threw a light
    behind,
Revealing to Olane the one for whom her spirit
    pined,
In his hand a knotty bludgeon, not improbably des-
    tined
    To silence any noisy foe about.
She saw him through a corner of the netted window-
    blind,
    And fancied he was grown a little stout.

Clarence threw away the match and puffed in great
    content,
While he thrummed a lame fandango on the
    wretched instrument.
After waking up the servants, he considerately
    went,
    And Hoodoo saw him safely out of sight.
Then he came beneath the window, and with
    guarded whisper, she
Convinced her much-bewildered brain that it was
    really he,
And the two arranged a rendezvous beneath the
    hollow tree,

By Elfin Bower on the morrow night.
He promising to meet her there, whenever he
should see
  The old familiar glimmer of the signal light.

Little did she sleep that night, her mind was in a
whirl,
And all next day she moved and spoke as when she
was a girl.
Clarence stared, and gave his weak mustache a
vicious twirl
  To see the roses gather on her cheek.
That night she stole out unobserved, and safely
pulled across,
And with Hoodoo had a hugging match, to com-
pensate a loss
Not worthy of description, people do not care a
toss
  For hysterical affection, so to speak ;
The history of a day would yield examples by the
gross
  In odd divorce, or suicidal freak.

He hid the boat along the bank in case Olane were
chased,
Threw a rope around a limb, the end about her
waist,
Both pulling on the other end, without unseemly
haste,
  She was hoisted to the hollow in the trunk ;

He showed her through the passage, now 'twas
    easy to traverse,
The roots were smoothly buried, and the spring,
    which ran perverse,
Dripping from the roof before, now went to reim-
    burse
  An earthen pitcher, broad and deep, within the
    passage sunk,
Led thereto by strips of bark ; the water was no
    worse,
  But perhaps a little cooler than the village people
    drunk.

When she entered Hoodoo's cavern, one may judge
    of her surprise,
Such a fairy transformation scene as lay before her
    eyes,
Each article of ancient ware a veritable prize,
  To Olane, who proceeded to inspect.
The pearls and rarer wampum were unusually
    fine,
And a million facets gleaming like the gems upon
    a shrine,
The grotto glittered brightly like Aladdin's jewel
    mine,
  From the crystals o'er the surface richly
    flecked ;
Hoodoo there as Harlequin and she as Colum-
    bine,
  With a singularly brilliant effect.

How they passed the time away is difficult to guess,
But one may judge it to have been in comfort more
      or less,
As 'twas midnight ere they parted, in a state of
      happiness
  No bachelor is able to describe ;
And Olane gliding onward in her boat across the
      water,
Resembled more a water nymph than Merley's only
      daughter.
If anyone had seen her there, 'tis what they would
      have thought her,
  For the rustics are a superstitious tribe.
She entered by the balcony ; experience had taught
      her
  That a servant knows the value of a bribe.

After this they grew more daring, and had both
      been seen together,
By a person who had heard about the hunter clad
      in leather,
And the negro, both of whom were drowned ; but
      failed to notice whether
  The smaller hooded figure was a male.
He scuttled to his family, forever after steer-
      ing
From the patch of land by Castle rocks, a lovely
      little clearing
Level as a shaven lawn, where spirits were appear-
      ing,

Who had tragically left this earthly vale.
The story reached the village, which was infinitely
 cheering :
 For the gossips dearly love a grisly tale.

Weeks had passed away, yet Merley suffered from
 the gout;
The doctor said he probably would never get about,
The disease had found the nursery from where it
 started out,
 Like a tired prodigal returning home ;
When gout attacks the stomach, like the prodigal
 it stays,
Or only leaves its quarters for a few uncertain days,
And presently the little home has vanished from
 our gaze,
 The prodigal will nevermore roam.
Old Merley made his testament, preparing, logic
 says,
 To become incorporated with the loam.

The property was left in trust for Clarence, to command
Until Olane saw convenient to render him her
 hand ;
In the meantime she was granted board and lodging, understand,
 Which in case of misalliance, was to cease ;
And the property was deeded to a charitable
 scheme

For providing pauper gentlefolks with tea and dairy
    cream ;
And to building a cathedral—even Merley had a
    dream
  Of procuring his salvation on a lease.
If the plan concerning Clarence and Olane should
    kick the beam,
  He bequeathed them each a quarter dollar piece.

He told his hopeful nephew of the way affairs were
    brewing,
So Clarence woke up suddenly, and saw he must
    be doing,
His powers of fascination were unequal to sub-
    duing
  The spirit of the lady he desired ;
But growing fairly desperate, he tremulously
    popped,
Or surely would have done, but that his utterance
    was stopped ;
Olane quietly told him that the theme were better
    dropped,
  And leaving him, indignantly retired ;
But he took a brandy cocktail, and, his resolution
    propped,
  Intruded in her chamber, passion fired.

She was putting on a hooded cloak, the lamp was
    on the sill,
A faint red light was visible from lake and
    gloomy hill ;

But when Clarence came she listened to his story
    of the will,
  Then contemptuously bade him to be gone;
But he acted so unpleasantly, at least, so rumor
    said,
That Olane seized the lamp and hit the villain o'er
    the head,
It bursting on the floor and setting fire to the
    bed,
  When Clarence, shorn of all his fanfaron,
Had sneaked away upstairs, while Olane had
    swiftly fled,
  So the fire in the chamber crackled on.

Hoodoo met his wife, and as he listened to her
    tale,
The anger settled in his heart, and left his features
    pale;
No evil word escaped his tongue, he knew not
    how to rail,
  But he let her climb the entrance to the cave;
Deliberately whetted up a lengthy hunting-knife,
And started over to the house, with murder run-
    ning rife.
In his temper, he had hidden, when they hunted
    for his life,
  Now he would deal according as they gave;
But a glare about the mansion showed a scene of
    busy strife,
  From Olane's window leapt a fiery wave.

Smoke was curling everywhere, along the man-
sion front,
And the servants did but little in the place, ex-
cept to hunt
For valuable trifles.   Merley's manner being blunt,
They were working for their wages, not for
love:
His room was on the second floor, but no one
seemed to fret
As to whether he was roasting, it was easy to for-
get.
Clarence usually slept a story higher yet.
The fire now was taking hold above,
And the flames were roaring fierce with innumer-
able jet,
While the zephyrs gave the tragedy a shove.

Hoodoo passed the villagers and people gathered
there,
Who viewed his resurrection with a horror-stricken
stare;
He made no explanation, there was little time to
spare.
The balcony he mounted at a bound,
Knowing how the passage ran, to get to Merley's
rooms,
Blindly rushed along to where the door dimly
looms,
Brought the old man groaning through the suf-
focating fumes,

Then inquired if the nephew were around.
Smoke was belching everywhere in black and fiery
    plumes
  Through the windows from the roof unto the
    ground.

All the population of the village stood and viewed,
Delighted with the show on domain heretofore
    tabooed,
But shrank away from Hoodoo with a quiet solici-
    tude,
  Whispering together of the ghost—
Of the disembodied negro in the sable flowing
    gown.
Hoodoo's face distorted by a diabolic frown,
A loaded pistol ready cock't, to shoot the nephew
    down ;
  But destiny annulled his savage boast,
His action saving Merley, even, brought him no re-
    nown,
  People said, 'twas not their time to roast.

So no one answered, nobody had anything to tell,
And Hoodoo watched the fire in the breezes
    grandly swell,
When from a lofty chimney-pot there came an
    awful yell,
  And all beheld emerge a sooty figure ;
Who sitting on the top, his feet adangle in the
    flue,
With mad gesticulation beat a horrible tattoo,

9

Laughed, and snapped, and jibbered like a crazy
    cockatoo,
  The people cried—the Spirit of the nigger:
And Hoodoo knowing Clarence, who had barely
    struggled through,
  Raving mad with terror, eased the trigger.

A crackle and a sputter from the heart of crimson
    flame.
Then together inward falling, both the roof and
    chimney came,
An upward rush of fiery sparks, and fragments of
    the frame;
  A sizzle, and a groaning from the mob.
Hoodoo went to Merley, who was breathing out
    his last,
Who apologized for injuries committed in the past,
And gave a dying blessing, for his breath was ebb-
    ing fast,
  When Olane, who was there, began to sob.
'Twas a most affecting scene, but as a rigid para-
    phrast,
  I consider I am over with the job.

Merley made no other will; his daughter did not
    care,
The other precious document was burned to ashes
    there,
And Hoodoo, as her husband, thus became the legal
    heir.
  The backbone of their miseries was gone:

And how he had a suit of clothes, by Olane's
    special wish
And how he thought himself a most confounded
    queer fish,
And how he tried to swear at the somewhat
    ticklish
    Sensation of a linen collar—on,
Is recorded in the chronicles of utter gibberish.
    It may be here—may be this is one.

Hoodoo and Olane were blest, in spite of all their
    sins,
And a crowd of ankle-biters, more than one of
    whom were twins,
But he—they never civilized, he wore mocassins,
    And rambled with his rifle through the wood:
The second generation are a race of sturdy men,
And their daughters are so fair as to paralyze my
    pen ;
Quality and quantity, they number nine or ten,
    And as far as I can learn are brave and good.
The sun is brightly shining on their fortunes now
    as then,
    Tho' they never boast of pedigree or blood.

But what they do is better for humanity at large ;
They treat their working people as a providential
    charge,
Nor spend their time and money on a gaudy pleas-
    ure barge,
    Or gaming with a parasitic crew ;

They never reared buildings to commemorate their
     name,
Their employees have never struck, to their eternal
     shame;
Decent profits hardly bear the philanthropic game,
    Which is played to great perfection by a screw.
And there I will leave them, to be burdened with
     the blame,
    If this parting panegyric be untrue.

The hollow tree and cavern I discovered and ex-
     plored
I found it richly furnished, and luxuriously stored
With every convenience; and now they can afford
    To use it as a rustic shooting-box;
And a member of the family, surprising me inside,
Accepted my apologies, and kindly gratified,
My thirst for information of the hunter and his
     bride,
    And how they had to hide in Castle Rocks;
And to this day they still conduct the chosen few
     with pride,
    To picnic in this hollow paradox.

They built another mansion on the slope between
     the hills,
Where a crystal streamlet bubbles, and the song-
     bird gayly trills,
And the forest grandly rises, here the pigeon fondly
     bills,
    While the squirrels frolic through the leafy glade;

A flowery meadow greenly rolling downward to
      the lake
Dotted o'er with sleeky kine, and frisky lambs who
      shake,
Their baby heads and aspen tails, at sheep, who
      half-awake,
   In woolly vacant reverie are strayed ;
And water-fowl jerk lamely through the reeds as
      they forsake,
   The rubbish where a cunning nest is made.

The village droning onward in the distance as of
      yore,
But a deeper dulness dawning, for old Brown is
      now no more,
And he lies in consecrated ground with grasses
      nodding o'er,
   To the chiming of the drowsy chapel bells,
Where many souls are summoned, and a few are
      gained, I hope,
On placid Sunday morn or eve, when rustic sinners
      grope,
Toward a purer state of things with prayer or
      mottled soap,
   According as the moral feeling dwells ;
And further curiosity will find an ample scope,
   In a visit to the land of Honeywells.

LEGEND OF THE TIDAL RIVER LEA.

PART FIRST.

REMOTELY known, on the English coast,
　Where the land lies low and level,
Dwells a rustic folk, whose leading toast
　In the not infrequent revel,
Is the river that flows from the sea inland,
Or ebbs as the ocean tides command,
Till a big ship floats, or the urchins stand,
　In the trail of a deep sea devil,
　　By a fable of ye olden time.

Tradition told of a mammoth snake,
　Of an instinct fierce and gory,
Which wallowed a way through the marshy brake,
　According to their story.
And here it basked in the sunny heat
For dinner devouring a maiden sweet,
Till a bold knight slew it ; the marvellous feat
　Obscured his name with glory,
　　From the battle of ye olden time.

The name of the village is little account,
　For it slipped my recollection ;
But the people yet have a fair amount
　Of my reverent affection ;

Sons or daughters to the sons of the sea,
Simple and honest as they well can be
In the land of the tidal river Lea,
   As I choose to name that section,
     For the sake of ye olden time.

Years ago to the sleepy port,
   Came a ship all worn and battered,
With a rollicking crew of a reckless sort,
   Her canvas torn and tattered;
The bulwarks gone, where the wild wave crashed,
And a howling tempest raving lashed,
When a driving spray o'er the sailors dashed,
   Till their locks with brine grew matted
     Like the beards of ye olden time.

She had braved the breakers along the shore,
   To the mouth of the tidal river;
'Twas a Yankee ship with wealth galore
   In the hands of the careless giver,
And the quiet little village rang ere long
To the deep-sea shandy, or roving song,
Rolling an echo, bold and strong,
   To the maiden ears aquiver
     With the glamour of the olden time.

The tars drank deep of the rarest brew,
   Till the light came faintly dawning;
They fought like furies, but fairly too,
   In the wee small hours of the morning,
Yet dusk in the evening found them true

To the faith of the moonlight rendezvous,
Mid the shadowy lanes and the falling dew,
   In the teeth of the graybeards' warning,
      As it happened in ye olden time.

Many a maiden fair and young,
   Merry with a playful passion,
Their guileless souls so finely strung
   In the key of the old-time fashion,
Which tells of the lover so bold and true,
Who sails away on the briny blue
With never a lady among the crew,
   And a temperate scale of ration,
      Like a saint of ye olden time.

In dove-like pairs they wandered forth,
   Through lanes they roved securely,
They spread to the eastward, west, and north,
   Their faces set demurely;
On the south lay the river, and the Yankee ship,
Whence two by two would the jack tars slip,
And away to the wandering maidens skip,
   Who were quite unawaring, surely,
      In the humor of ye olden time.

There Pippin of the foretop, short and stout,
   Muscular, hard, and hairy,
Was taken aback when he wandered out
   By a sweet-faced maid named Mary;
Tubs of the forecastle swore by Jane,

Chips and a Lilly agreed in the grain,
And Grace found Parsons in mental pain,
  While the rhymer of the ship saw a fairy
    As fair as in ye olden time.

'Twas the rhyming tar, with a beardless chin,
  And the theories glibly spoken,
Of the endless trouble he tumbled in,
  And a short pug nose twice broken ;
The bandied limbs, and the tousled hair,
Who sang of the mermaids wondrous fair,
While the crew chimed in with a chorus rare,
  And he led them by that token,
    Like a troop of ye olden time.

By a gray old church, with the big square tower,
  Where bells rung sweet and sadly,
By the quaint old inn where the fragrant flower
  Made the lovelorn heart ache badly ;
The ruined old abbey where the ivy climbs,
In the dells, where the blackbird trills at times,
Were fond hearts echoing the mystic chimes,
  Which made wise men do madly,
    As was ever in ye olden time.

When the clock in the tower boomed half-past
    ten,
  With a strain of moral rancor,
Then the maidens murmured adieu to the men,
  Who glowered a hopeless canker,

They pleaded vainly, the maid soon gone,
And a light in her chamber window shone,
Drifting disconsolate, one by one
   They gathered at the sign of the Anchor,
     A tavern of ye olden time.

A fisherman's daughter can deftly row
   The skiff where the wavelet shimmers,
Her voice makes music to the old banjo
   Where the moon, reflected, glimmers,
Her eyes are luminous with subtle light,
As his voice floats musical love through the night,
And the chords magnetically throb with delight,
   For the soul of the rhymer simmers
     With a fervor of ye olden time.

But the fair young dove flies home to roost,
   At the sound of the half-hour booming,
The eloquent tongue of the lover unloosed
   Is tied by a futile fuming ;
For the boat scrapes harshly along the shore,
One stolen kiss, and the dream is o'er,
And she disappears, to be seen no more,
   Till the morrow in the twilight glooming,
     Like a vision of ye olden time.

Mournfully up by the stone bridge wall,
   With the banjo slung right handy,
He meets with his shipmates, short and tall,
   But all their legs look bandy.

Then a generous bout with the nut-brown purl,
The tars in turn toast the Unseen Girl,
Then march where the river's eddyings whirl,
  Refraining the deep sea shandy,
    In the manner of ye olden time.

The banjo twangs with a sounding pank
  As the leading voice goes pealing,
Down a silent street, to the river bank,
  Where a misty veil is stealing ;
And an echo floats it back again,
Like a distant hail from the briny main ;
The tars join in with a wierd refrain,
  And a hurricane of feeling,
    In a tune of ye olden time.

SHANDY.

Sing roving far o'er the briny water,
  Aye, ho, boys, roll and go,
None so fair as a sailor's daughter
  Carry me along to my own true love ;
Her eyes are a light for the homeward bounder,
A fair breeze travelling lingers round her
Follow, my lads, till the winds have found her,
  Ransome, sweetheart, ransome me.

There's storm in the distance fiercely growling,
  Aye, ho, boys, roll and go ;
But I hear her sigh thro' the tempest howling
  Carry me along to my own true love,

The waves may roar, and the thunders rumble
None but she may find me humble,
Down in her lap my gold shall tumble,
    Ransome, sweetheart, ransome me.

For a buzzing breeze in the ratlines moaning,
    Aye, ho, boys, roll and go ;
A bubbling wake, and the timbers groaning,
    Carry me along to my own true love,
Bellow in the sail, o'er the old tub skating,
Rattle in the rigging and clatter on the grating,
Hurry me along to a fair maid waiting,
    Ransome, sweetheart, ransome me.

Swift with the tide in the channel rushing,
    Aye, ho, boys, roll and go,
Sheet set taut with a fair wind pushing,
    Carry me along to my own true love ;
High in the window a faint light twinkles,
A chorus bold, as the banjo tinkles,
Merry little maiden, smooth these wrinkles,
    Ransome, sweetheart, ransome me.

———

And as the band went trolling down the road,
    At certain intervals a gentle flutter,
Behind the diamond panes and curtain showed,
    While some one's voice betrayed an eager stutter,
The maiden, roused by the strain she hears,
Has two bright eyes suffused with tears,
Her soft young soul is beset with fears,
    Too vague for the tongue to utter,
        Like a seeress of ye olden time.

The dried old gaffers totter out of beds,
    With click and creak of windows open swinging ;
Grannies popping out their nightcapt heads,
    Would squawk a shaky quaver to the singing ;
Doddering old sailors, waiting quietly for the grave,
Their brawny sons now absent on the bosom of the
        wave,
Bellow feebly in the shandy while their grizzled
     whiskers wave,
    Their memory pathetically winging
      To the frolic of ye olden time.

The watchmen list to the billowy sound
    They join in the odd procession,
And join when the sweet refrain comes round
    For they sing with great expression ;
Their stern looks gradually grow less grim,
The melody makes their eyes grow dim,
But they swell the chorus with a fanatic vim,
    Like sinners at confession,
      To a friar of ye olden time.

The lord of the manor passes by
    But never a hat was lifted,
He scowls on them with lowering eye,
    For a tale has widely drifted
Of the woman who lives in the ivied cot
Her fair fame smirched with a lifelong blot ;
But the lord of the manor heeds her not,
    Her shame may never be lifted,
      Which befell her in ye olden time.

No happier maiden lived, one day,
   In the village of the shining water,
Than the bonny dark-eyed laughing fay
   Who was known as the fisherman's daughter
Years gone by, for the seasons go,
As the tidal waters ebb and flow.
Now her raven locks in the breezes blow,
    And a wisdom time has taught her
      By the trouble of ye olden time.

Her face is fair, and her eyes shine bright,
   Her mellow voice rings sweetly,
Her step is springing yet, and light,
   And her garments clinging neatly.
She lives alone, with a daughter fair
Of the same soft eyes, and silky hair,
And, friend or foe, there are none may share,
    In the secret kept discreetly,
      Of the doings of ye olden time.

Her father sails his fishing smack
   To the banks of the briny ocean ;
He brings her curious trifles back,
   But the child has a fancied notion,
That his eyes grow dark as he scans her face,
For the well-known traits of a reckless race,
Then the harsh lines soften to her winsome grace,
    And a kindlier emotion,
      Which is not of ye olden time.

The mother takes her along to church,
   Each peaceful Sunday morning,

And of late the rhyming tar would lurch,
  To sit in the background yawning;
Then home to her door he beguiled their way,
With the fun that a sailor alone can say,
And she finds it awkward to say him nay,
  In the light of the new love dawning
    From the sorrows of ye olden time.

Yet she gives him to know she has once been wed,
  Tho' the proof thereof is missing,
That she waits till her scampish spouse be dead,
  Her voice with hatred hissing.
And he seeks to discover the rascal's name,
That his blood may cleanse her life from shame,
But she held her peace, so that all which came,
  From the theme was an ardent kissing
    In defiance of ye olden time.

PART SECOND.

In the smithy by the landing lived a gray-
    beard hale and hearty,
  His rosy face resembling some ancient figure-
    head,
He was dignified in bearing, and of no uncertain
    standing
  Like the famous Bonaparte, who by wit and wis-
    dom led,
He was deft as a mechanic, with the lore of his
    trade

By the mystery vulcanic, he a cosey living made,
His head was long and level, and his soul was not
　　　afraid,
　　As he labored in the smithy by the tidal river
　　　Lea.

He was favored by the pastor of the church so
　　　gray and ancient,
　　Where the tombstones gleam out whitely from
　　　amid the rustling trees ;
And his forge sent out a clamor as he welded calm
　　　and patient
　　With the sparkles flying swiftly and the bellows'
　　　angry wheeze.
The fisherman returning with a scaly silvern spoil,
Marked the ruddy flare burning and tumultous
　　　turmoil,
And was fain to rest his muscles after weary hours
　　　of toil,
　　In the smithy of the village by the tidal river
　　　Lea.

People called him Benny Rowland, from a liking
　　　that they bore him ;
　　Of manner bright and genial, to everyone alike.
They who settled there before him, said he wan-
　　　dered from the lowland,
　　When his homestead was demolished by the
　　　bursting of a dyke.
A baby girl of tender years, which tenderly he
　　　carried

Was all he had, the mother had been drowned
    where'er she tarried,
And was later found and buried by the chapel
    where they married,
    E'er they settled in the lowland of the tidal river
      Lea.

He had prospered in his calling by a sturdy perse-
    verance,
    And the crippled Yankee vessel brought him
      gear to repaïr,
By a youth of good appearance, when the shades
    of night were falling,
    Who could tell a tragic story how the vessel
      drifted there.
He was bo'sun of the damaged craft, a boon com-
    panion too,
And in their cot enjoyed a draught of strong Oc-
    tober brew.
So it fell that Marie Rowland and the handsome
    bo'sun grew
    Well acquainted in the village by the tidal river
      Lea.

She had grown to be a beauty in their homely little
    dwelling,
    As a violet might blossom by some rugged bowl-
      der's side,
And he heard her father telling of the maiden's
    loving duty,
10

With a curious conviction that she was his fu-
ture bride,
From her hand a fervid feeling set his inner soul
a-tingle,
Their furtive glances stealing seemed to magically
mingle
On his ear her voice with melody magnetic seemed
to jingle,
While the maiden when he answered softly
sighed,
In the cottage of the village by the tidal river
Lea.

And thereafter in the gloaming by the footpath
o'er the moor,
Stood a sunburnt sailor watching for the lovely
earnest face,
Where the moonlight calmly pours while the
stricken ones are roaming,
The presence of each other sanctifying time and
place,
Of the world they little wondered in their strange
infatuation ;
Even destiny had blundered in the vessel's desti-
nation.
And brought them to a spot replete with every
fascination,
That Nature can afford the human race,
In that solitary village by the tidal river
Lea.

Benny Rowland, unsuspecting of the way affairs
      were going,
  Saw the happy pair roving, with a calm un-
      shaken trust,
Far adown the river rowing; and he lent without
      reflection
  Their tiny boat, whose anchor chain was thick
      with idle rust;
For his lordship of the manor once had met a chill
      rebuff,
When the maiden had been pestered by his ogling
      enough,
And appealed to Benny Rowland, who had spoken
      very rough,
  To the scion of an ancient upper crust,
    Whilom rulers of the village by the tidal river
    Lea.

A libertine with power, in the shape of lands and
      money,
  A God upon a bicycle his loftiest ideal;
Of some bucolic cleverness, impertinently funny,
  And a dignity of bearing, either gross or fune-
      real;
A magistrate, by virtue of his standing in the shire,
But secretly a gambler, a drunkard, also liar;
Ambitious as old Satan with libidinous desire,
  And he cast a look of envy on the lovers' true
      and leal,
    As they wandered in the meadows by the tidal
    river Lea.

And in spite of their traditions there were very few
    revered him,
  For his record as a gentleman was ominously
    dark,
In their hearts a many hated, and the balance
    vaguely feared him,
  While his tenants all reported him a veritable
    shark.
When the daughter of the fisherman had wandered
    home again,
With her baby girl o'ershadowed by a miserable
    stain,
She kept her story hidden in her now enlightened
    brain,
  Lest her fond old father make a fatal mark,
    On the villain of the village by the tidal river
    Lea.

But she cursed him when she met him, with the
    fervor of a prophet,
  And he listened as he hurried from the injured
    woman's path,
Saying, 'ere he went to Tophet, that the Lord might
    not forget him,
  But inflict a retribution in the righteousness of
    wrath ;
And a chill foreboding shiver sent a tremor thro'
    his frame.
While deeming weakling innocence a fascinating
    game,
He rarely felt compunction for the misery or shame

Of his victim in the hopeless aftermath—
  But the vengeance of the elders of the tidal
    river Lea!

The Yankee ship was lying on the bank across the
    ferry,
  And the carpenters had torn away the bo'sun's
    private bunk;
The sailors making merry made the situation try-
    ing,
  Occasionally some of them would get extremely
    drunk;
So the bo'sun, rather tired of the gay nocturnal
    din,
Which is not to be desired after one has tumbled
    in,
With a dreamy recollection of the fair transparent
    skin
  Of a saintly vision, beaming on a monk,
    Hired a chamber at the Anchor by the tidal
      river Lea.

A rambling old ruin, once a pleasant country villa,
  Massy walls and windows, with the lattice dia-
    mond paned,
An enormous weeping-willow o'er the door one en-
    tered through in,
  And a mossy thatch by many years of weather
    darkly stained,
But the landlord was so jolly, and so corpulent to
    boot,

The bare idea was folly that the quarters wouldn't
    suit ;
The inn for some four hundred years had held a
    good repute,
    Tho' it may have leaked a trifle when it rained
      On the houses of the village by the tidal river
    Lea.

Inside a sandy flooring showed an excavated hollow,
    Worn by generations of the hobnailed British
    shoe,
Which was excellent to follow for the visitor ex-
    ploring,
    To the cosiest old parlor that a traveller ever
    knew.
From a huge cavernous chimney came a warm and
    ruddy glare,
On the oaken wainscot firmly flanked by weighty
    bench or chair,
Deep corroded by the ravages that time had eaten
    there ;
    The ceiling raftered ponderously too,
      As was common in the village by the tidal
    river Lea.

Here the shadows nod and flicker where the rug-
    ged seamen gather,
    Where the pudding-featured pot-boy passed the
    potent home-brew'd ale,
With a crown of creamy lather, and they sip the
    honest liquor

From the pewter, as a knotty-faced old sailor tells
    a tale,
In a dialect besprinkled with the phrasing of the
    sea,
And a leathern forehead wrinkled by the strain of
    memory,
With a horny finger lifted as they listen earnestly,
    Of the time that he was shipwrecked in a gale,
      Long remembered in the village by the tidal
      river Lea.

Here the clock whereon a rooster stood, defiantly
    and ready,
    As depicted by the artist, to victoriously crow;
Ill-natured rumor said he was an emblem of the
    brewster,
    The only "tick" available was swinging to and
    fro.
Tho' his smile was sweet as honey, it was tacitly
    believed
That a dearth of ready money was the only sin he
    grieved,
His twinkling little vision was too keen to be de-
    ceived,
    A winding-up made clock and business go,
      In the cosey little parlor by the tidal river Lea.

The landlord's pretty daughter, lightly here and
    there flitting
    On the business of the sanctum where the higher
    caste repair,

Which is surely very fitting, for the sailor is a
    snorter,
  Where a merchant gravely listens with a self-
    complacent air.
Jane had watched the bo'sun with an absent-minded
    stare,
Who saw that her complexion was unusually
    fair;
Then she fell a willing victim to sensations sweet
    and rare,
  When he kissed her, which of course he had not
    ought to,
    In the tavern of the village by the tidal river
    Lea.

But the bo'sun's purse was weighty, and the host
    displayed a chamber
  Of ghastly air, but many rare old pictures on the
    wall,
Where a pretty girl was smiling on a veteran of
    eighty,
  Who was scowling at the bo'sun with the bitter-
    ness of gall;
A warrior with ringlets aimed a dire destructive
    jab,
At a convict clad in singlets of unutterable drab,
Who had just fired off a blunderbuss and waited
    for the stab
  From a rapier, which never seemed to fall,
    In the picture of the chamber by the tidal river
    Lea.

Here Apollyon scared a pedler, who with apoplectic
    vision,
  Rubbed his hands in feeble protest at the mon-
    ster's merry grin,
Indicating with precision, that the demon was a
    meddler,
  And whatever his pretension it was evidently
    thin.
Whene'er the bo'sun went to bed, he scanned this
    work of art,
But the morning had not altered the position of the
    dart.
The speculation might have racked a nervous per-
    son's heart,
  As to whether he—the pedler—saved his skin ;
    But the bo'sun slumbered soundly by the tidal
    river Lea,

On the quaking bog of feathers, in the carven mam-
    moth coffin,
  With a canopy suspended overhead, of massive
    oak ;
And he promptly glided off into a dream of forty
    wethers,
  Round a lamb with Marie's features, who was
    telling them a joke ;
Then a serpent gliding stealthily had poised a
    venomed fang,
When a ram with long gray whiskers struck the
    scaly head a bang,

Which sounded as a hammer on the smithy anvil
　　　rang,
　　And the whole affair vanished as he woke,
　　　In the chamber of the Anchor by the tidal river
　　　Lea.

On the chamber threshold waiting, with his hand
　　　upon the handle,
　　Stood the landlord of the Anchor with an anx-
　　　ious puckered brow
Holding up a flaring candle, who began by blandly
　　　stating
　　That his hostelry was crowded to the fullest limit
　　　now.
The yearly celebration of the customary fair
Increased the population till they had no room to
　　　spare,
And the lord of all the manor waited on the landing
　　　there.
　　Belated in the village of the tidal river Lea.

'Twas early in the morning and the rain was wildly
　　　pouring,
　　The manor lay some distance by a dark and
　　　muddy road,
Its people soundly snoring, barred and bolted till
　　　the morning,
　　And in praise of early rising, then a chanticleer
　　　crowed.
His lordship wished to share his bed, the largest in
　　　the place.

The bo'sun ignorantly said he understood the case,
Was delighted to oblige him, with a hospitable
grace
In the chamber of the tavern by the tidal river
Lea.

And his lordship waxing jolly at the turn it gave
affairs
Made an ample explanation of the circumstances
that
Are a fertile source of pairs, just a little youthful
folly,
And dilated on the beauties of a game at baccarat.
The bo'sun did not care, so returned the fair ad-
vances,
By a promise to be there and investigate the
chances
At eleven on the morrow night, when fashionable
dances
In society are opened, few are earlier than that,
Not counting in the village by the tidal river
Lea.

On the morrow, after Marie from their trysting
place departed,
He repaired to his appointment at the hour of
eleven,
Feeling very tender-hearted, for to-night his blushing fairy
Had decided she would marry him to crystallize
their heaven.

So the landlord led the way into a private little den.
But the bo'sun could not play, which plainly
thunderstruck the men,
So the detail of description is denied my rhyming
pen,
For their tactics were unusually wary,
In the layout of the tavern by the tidal river
Lea.

On a sideboard were decanters, also wines of varied
vintage,
Beneath a painted abigail of most peculiar mien,
Whose eyes betrayed a squintage, like a pair of
vigilantes
Charging bayonets in a riot, both were uniformly
green.
To the young commercial drummer who was losing
all his cash,
Jane administered a hummer of the whiskey labeled
Mash,
And the bo'sun drank sufficient to become ex-
tremely rash,
Had he understood the motive of the scene,
In the little tavern parlor by the tidal river **Lea.**

The charming Jane was playing a piano low and
sweetly
With musical ability one hardly would expect,
Attired very neatly, and occasionally saying
Merry trifles to the bo'sun which were more than
correct,

Or arranged the shining glasses as each named his
      pet potation,
And the potent fluid passes to promote exhilaration,
Till the bo'sun, growing reckless, stole a furtive os-
      culation,
    From the siren of the Anchor by the tidal river
      Lea.

She smiled on his caressing with an appetite for
      more,
    And he marked a fervent feeling blazing plainly
      in her eye;
The diamond that she wore in the cincture of her
      tresses,
    Shot a fiery rainbow sparkle, like her favor,
      nothing shy.
His pulse beat like a hammer, and his brain began
      to whirl,
From the sympathetic glamour of that tender-heart-
      ed girl,
Or the steaming whiskey toddy after sundry mugs
      of purl,
    From the barrel in the cellar by the tidal river
      Lea.

He told her she was pretty, which was welcome
      news to hear,
    By the pinky hue that deepened on the round
      transparent cheek,
And another glass of toddy filled his noble heart
      with pity,

That a previous engagement made it dangerous
    to speak.
The party cut and shuffled as it came unto their turn
Their hair wildly ruffled, but with faces set and stern,
While the coin chinked or jingled in the little silver
    urn,
    To be captured by some seeming lucky freak,
        Of the gamblers in the tavern by the tidal river
        Lea.

Boniface was playing with the drummer quite
    sedately,
    Against a local lawyer and his lordship, tho' they
        lost;
But he played deliberately, fate is fickle, he was
    saying,
    And the liquor circulated quite regardless of the
        cost;
So the drummer lost his coin, and despairing went
    to bed,
Departing on the morrow with a heavy aching head,
And was punished for embezzlement, a flying rumor
    said,
    While the bo'sun o'er the ferry slowly crossed,
        Rather weary of the tavern by the tidal river
        Lea.

The trio went carousing, each according to his
    planet,
    His lordship and mine host agreed the bo'sun
        was a fool,

And they gave the pretty Janet, tho' her father
    had been losing,
  A douceur in token of her knack for keeping
    cool,
Who repaired to the smithy, later on into the day
And had an artful gossip with old Benny by the way,
Who warned the handsome bo'sun that his manner
    was too gay,
  For the beauty of the village by the tidal river
    Lea.

He abused him somewhat coarsely, and the fisher
    people hearkened
  For a challenge from the bo'sun, they were both
    about a size,
But his features only darkened, as he said, good
    morning, hoarsely,
  Meeting Marie by the ferry to his gratified sur-
    prise;
Then he made a full confession, and the girl was
    satisfied
That he meant no slack affection for his late affi-
    anced bride,
There they settled on a meeting by the haunted
    mere side,
  Very early in the morning, down the tidal river
    Lea.

PART THIRD.

There's a mighty spreading oak, in the meadow
　　down the road,
Where the rocks afford a shelter to the bright-
　　eyed dingy toad,
There a stagnant pool of water o'er a pit has over-
　　flowed,
　　　　On the border of the lowland,
　　　　Sinking in the lowlands low.

It is said that spirits hover o'er the green unhealthy
　　scum,
And that water witches gather here to brew in-
　　fernal rum,
That deep below the surface many bones are lying
　　dumb,
　　　　From the flooding of the lowlands,
　　　　Sunk into the lowlands low.

By the tidal river bounded, to or from the ocean
　　sweeping,
An artificial levee held the land in safer keeping,
When the tide came breaking through it, there
　　was misery and weeping,
　　　　'Mid the settlers of the lowland,
　　　　Toiling in the lowlands low.

It was here that Benny Rowland built a tiny little
　　cot,
And reclaimed a goodly portion of a twenty-acre lot,

Till the sea came madly rushing o'er the well-
    remembered spot,
        Bringing ruin to the lowlands,
        And mourning in the lowlands low.

A narrow path goes winding by the oak and up
    the hill,
Through a tangling of undergrowth, where all is
    calm and still,
Save the trickle of some garrulous, but limpid lit-
    tle rill,
        Running down into the lowlands,
        To sink in the lowlands low.

Grassy banks on either side where violets thickly
    grow,
Or the dainty primrose clusters, where the sum-
    mer breezes blow,
Here there ran a noisy brooklet, in the ages long
    ago,
        To the marshes of the lowlands,
        To mingle in the lowlands low.

Down the levee from the village, one fine morning
    bright and fair,
Came old Benny Rowland's daughter, with the
    shining raven hair,
To the oak tree by the haunted pool, to meet her
    lover there,
        For a journey through the lowland
        To the pastor of the lowlands low.

11

Some idle scandal monger with a tongue of ve-
    nomed talent,
Belied the bo'sun sorely as an evil-meaning gal-
    lant.
Her father had insulted him, which turned the final
    balance
        For a wedding in the lowlands,
        In the chapel of the lowlands low.

They met and fondly wrestled to prolong the
    salutation,
Which circumstance appeared to enhance the situ-
    ation,
While the birds were piping joyously, with subtle
    penetration,
        Of the drama in the lowlands,
        Enacted in the lowlands low.

Thro' the wood they went together, where the
    sunlight flashes brightly,
Thro' the leaves which rustle o'er, as the fairies
    whisper quietly,
Where the bluebell and the hyacinth are flirting
    somewhat tritely,
        In the shadows of the lowland,
        On the border of the lowlands low.

O'er a style of rude construction, down a lane of
    leafy hedges,
Where fragrant honeysuckle or the wiry bramble
    wedges;

O'er a bridge, across a weedy swamp, of rushy
    growing sedges,
        Draining over to the lowland,
        Straining through the lowlands low.

By the spring of magic virtue, ever cool and lim-
    pid dripping,
Which insures the fond enamoured ones from
    accidental slipping.
They honor the tradition by a momentary sipping,
        Then hurry to the lowlands,
        To marry in the lowlands low.

Past the wayside inn, where carven in the stone
    above the door,
In the olden English lettering, are mottoes three
    or four,
And a crumbling glass and bottle, of the misty
    days of yore,
        When the tide was on the lowlands,
        Or ebbing from the lowlands low.

Up a hill and down another, where the grain was
    greenly waving,
By a clump of sturdy hemlock, where the rooks
    are ever raving,
A colony whose twig-built homes, the wind and
    weather braving
        Have a view of all the lowlands ;
        They forage in the lowlands low.

To the chapel on a hillock, and a tiny cottage ris-
ing,
Here the silver-haired old prophet did the week-
ly sermonizing,
Splicing lovers who were stranded, and their prog-
eny baptizing,
For the settlers in the lowland,
Who labor in the lowlands low.

He listened as the bo'sun and his sweetheart told
the story,
His fine old face encircled by a silver flowing
glory,
Then he read the marriage service, from his ancient
repertory,
And he blessed them in the lowland,
As they left him in the lowlands low.

The newly wedded lovers while the day was at its
best,
Took the turnpike o'er the highland, but remained
awhile to rest,
In a little wayside cottage, quaint with old-time in-
terest,
On the borders of the lowland,
Which overlooks the lowlands low.

An ancient couple hobbled on the yellow sandy
floor,
Their rosy wrinkled faces with a welcome brim-
ming o'er,

For the happy-looking pair, in the little candy store,
    Where urchins of the lowlands,
    Squandered pennies of the lowland low.

Here the bo'sun bought a package, of an infinite
    variety,
And every youngster met that day, received a
    fair moiety,
Probably considered as a fad of high society
    When visiting the lowlands
    By the people of the lowlands low.

They wandered in the garden, which was gay with
    many flowers,
Where the good old gaffer labored to the limit of
    his powers,
Admired the vines and roses on the funny little
    bowers,
    And the honey of the lowlands,
    Gathered in the lowlands low.

They were shown three generations of a sleek do-
    mestic pussy,
A grandam and her daughter, who were purring
    proudly fussy,
As they suckled seven kittens, each a bold ma-
    ternal hussy,
    But a feline of the lowlands,
    The rovers of the lowlands low.

In the huge old-fashioned oven, now disused for
    many a year,

They had found two healthy litters squeaking hun-
    grily and clear;
The youngest generation was the one they chose
    to rear,
        For the terror of the lowlands
        Are vermin from the lowlands low.

How the dim old eyes did flicker as they bared
    their toothless gums,
While the fluffy little midgets hunted friskily for
    crumbs,
And they stared at the payment for the purchased
    sugar plums,
        That the children of the lowlands
        Might be merry in the lowlands low.

Backward looking when they parted, where the
    roof showed red and hollow,
The jutting eaves a shelter for the mortared nest
    of swallow,
When the old folks waved a towel while their dim
    old eyes could follow
        Down the highway of the lowlands,
        Skirting by the lowlands low.

A cut across a meadow and a pathway by a wood,
Where sleek, contented cattle chew a philosophic
    cud,
Little recking of the future and the shedding of
    their blood
        By the butchers of the lowlands,
        Who prosper in the lowlands low.

Peering in the forest glades for vaguely cherished
    risk,
Where long-eared rabbits rustle and the squirrels
    keenly whisk,
And pigs as black as Erebus alternate root or frisk,
      As they ramble to the lowlands,
      Or wander in the lowlands low.

They startle in a scamper, and a headlong rushing
    crackle—
The nose of every porker there is innocent of
    shackle—
But a monster boar opposes a formidable obstacle
      To the pair from the lowlands,
      United in the lowlands low.

His face is long and massive, and his nose is broad
    and blunt,
His ears are prodigious and nearly meet in front,
And gleaming yellow tushes emphasize a warning
    grunt
      From the monarch of the lowlands,
      Who wallows in the lowlands low.

They leave him to his dignity beneath the spread-
    ing beech,
Which was better manifestly for the happiness of
    each,
For a newly married couple or a boar are hard to
    teach,
      Be it either in the lowlands
      Or other than the lowlands low.

They clamber o'er another stile, and out across the
    moor,
The manor lies between them and the tidal river
    shore,
Beyond is seen the village, with the belfry rising
    o'er:
        Their visit to the lowlands,
        Recorded in the lowlands low.

PART FOUR.

Benny Rowland had arisen with the lark
    To arrange for the business of the day,
And he strode down the street with an echo to his
    feet
    As the far horizon shone a pearly gray.
A grand old man was Benny, tall and upright as
    a dart,
Taciturn in manner, but withal of kindly heart.
About an hour later on, his daughter made a start,
    For this morning ushered in her wedding-day,
But of that she kept her counsel, she had studied
    out her part,
    And required no other prompter in the play.

Benny labored in the smithy till the noon,
    Returning for his dinner, to the cot.
The meal was lying ready, but phenomenally soon,
    And beside it lay an empty pewter pot.
The maiden was not visible, and tho' an anxious
    thrill

Made his stout old heart grow heavy, very much
    against his will,
He reasoned that she went to gather herbs upon
    the hill,
    Which accounted for the meal not being hot,
So he took the pewter measure down the cellarway
    to fill
    It foaming from a barrel of the best that could
    be got.

Then he went to the smithy back again,
    And labored till the dusk of evening fell,
When he casually ran into the company of Jane,
    Who had something on her mind she wished to
    tell,
For she loved the jolly bo'sun with a love exceed-
    ing true,
And had guessed the haunted pool to be their
    secret rendezvous,
So vengefully she furnished Benny Rowland with
    the clue,
    Making furious emotion in him swell;
Yet he kept a prudent silence till the evening meal
    was through,
    And determined he would dissipate the spell.

Marie marked the grim suspicion in his look,
    As morosely he surveyed the simple fare,
Omitting to be merry on her merits as a cook,
    Which was something most peculiarly rare.
Then he silently arose, and strode away into the
    night,

Where a ragged, cloudy drift obscured Cynthia's
    friendly light
And she waited for her husband, in an agony of
    fright,
    The rosy hue her bonny face forsook,
While the wind arising gustily with chilly, sullen
    might
    Smote the cottage till the tiny building shook.

But the bo'sun came precisely at the hour,
    And clasped her in a pair of loving arms :
The indefinable terror from that moment had no
    power
    To arouse her tender soul in wild alarms ;
They waited till the morning showed a streak of
    livid gray,
But the foot of Benny Rowland never sounded on
    the way.
With sinister presentiments the wedded pair lay,
    A prey to many conscientious qualms,
Tho' in certain hopeful intervals it moveth me to say
    That the gloomy situation had its charms.

Then they lit the kitchen fire, and prepared
    A collation from whatever they could find,
And made a hearty breakfast, tho' the little wife
    was scared,
    While the bo'sun seemed a trifle more resigned.
He left her in the cottage, to report himself aboard,
Told the captain he was married to the lady he
    adored,

And the crew with sudden ecstasy so jubilantly
    roared
  That the rhymer in a hogshead was confined ;
But he bellowed through the bunghole of a theory
    all ignored,
  That the God of Love is veritably blind.

The captain, like a hero, gave the word,
  And the bo'sun piped all hands for extra grog,
The rhymer liberated that his banjo might be
    heard,
  And a holiday was entered on the log.
Someone set his wits to work and studied out a
    plan
To celebrate the wedding of their brother sailor-
    man,
And schemed the biggest racket, since the universe
    began,
  Had ever graced the lowland catalogue,
Which met vociferous applause, the novel notion
    ran
  Through the vessel like a can behind a dog.

The captain laid a shiny stove-pipe hat
  On the capstan, and the tars went lurching
    past,
And loaned the thriftless rhymer half a sovereign,
    so that
  He might muster with the " men " before the
    mast ;
Every sailor told the girl, who told a dozen more,

Who made their sweethearts agitate the enter-
    prise ashore.
The village school was voted, till the great event
    was o'er,
    While contributions came in thick and fast.
A grand piano standing in a corner of the floor
    Was the mite a charming widow lent the ball-
    room at the last.

The steward and the chef for once agreed,
    And evolved a rather lavish bill of fare,
Laid out nicely in the infant school, against the
    time of need,
    And the exhibition made the people stare.
The sailors scrubbed the boards of the floor clean
    and white,
Then waxed-and-turpentined until it glistened won-
    drous bright ;
Flags festooning gayly hid the bare walls from
    sight ;
    All the sailors clad in uniform were there ;
While a host of Chinese lanterns furnished many-
    colored light,
    And the tars were well instructed not to swear.

A wagon-load of flowers and evergreens,
    Whiskey, brandy, gin, and ginger-pop,
Lemonade and sandwiches, with Boston pork and
    beans,
    The contributions never seemed to stop ;

The infant school invaded by the trestle-work and
    chairs
Set with great diversity of many-fashioned wares,
Bonbons, fruit and flowers, still arriving up the
    stairs,
    Borrowed, begged, or purchased at the shop,
The jolly sailors waiting on the throng that capered
    there
In the intervals between each lively hop.

A piano made the music echo grand
    When persuaded by the village organist;
Young Harold, with an old Cremona fiddle, smil-
    ing bland,
    Swayed the dancers by the cunning of his wrist.
The village in its Sunday garb had entered in the
    fun,
The sailors showed their sweethearts how the fig-
    ures should be done,
One universal grin among the dancers seemed to
    run,
    E'en the spinsters were most liberally kissed;
And the captain's nose grew redder as he glorious-
    ly spun,
    Till a drop of perspiration on it hissed.

The dominie was capering with glee,
    The sexton grew hilarious for once;
The choristers, conspicuously out upon the spree,
    Were flirting with refreshing eloquence;

The aged people gazing on the scene of whirling
    vanity,
Occasionally stricken by a species of insanity,
One wild phantasmagoria of chuckling humanity,
    Where no one but a cripple was a dunce ;
A big bass viol droning with a musical urbanity,
    Or guffawing in short delirious grunts.

There might have been a famine in the land
    By the way in which the dainties disappeared,
And a corpulent old lady with a bottle in her hand
    Was said to be phenomenally cheered ;
Then the landlord of the Anchor sang a free and
    easy song,
With sly gesticulation and exposure of the tongue,
And the cheering when he finished was uproar-
    iously long ;
Then the rhymer, who was moderately beered,
Sang the favorite Old Shandy with a chorus wild
    and strong,
    And the general effect was something weird.

After finishing the vocal exercise,
    The captain of the vessel made a speech,
When he said the large attendance was a heavenly
    surprise,
    That his heart was full of more than he could
    preach ;
Then alluded to the bo'sun's hurried wedding as
    the cause
Of this tribute to the little god, of omnipresent laws,

When involuntary rapture opened wide the public
    jaws,
    And they cheered in an ear-splitting screech.
So the skipper, much elated in his spirit, had to
    pause,
    Aware that his voice would never reach.

When the cataclysm of ecstasy had died,
    He professed an ardent passion for the sex,
Their beauty paralyzed him with a paroxysm of
    pride,
    As he wiped a furtive tear from his specs ;
Said Memory would evermore cherish this event,
Thanking one and everybody for accommodation
    lent.
Then he called upon the bo'sun, as the time was
    nearly spent.
    But a queer fact transpired to perplex—
The bo'sun was not there, no one saw him as he went,
    But his absence was an incident to vex.

A few old people made a short address,
    The final anthem sung by one and all,
And the school-room was deserted in a twinkling
    or less,
    Wending homeward as the couples chanced to
    fall.
The rhymer saw his charmer to her door safe and
    sound,
Making love with desperation, o'er the intervening
    ground,

Who granted him permission, when his fortune
    came around,
  To marry her—the privilege was small.
And the twitter of the sparrows was the most
    resonant sound
  In the dawning of the morning of the ball.

Early in the night the bo'sun left,
  For Marie's anxious fears made him sad,
Her father's disappearance made her feel as if bereft
  Of the only real friend she ever had;
And that morn a local farmer, as he passed the
    haunted pool,
To take away some ware he had loaned the vil-
    lage school,
Fished a hat from off the surface, which he carried
    like a fool
  To the cottage, leaving Marie nearly mad,
For she knew it by the accidental branding of a
    tool,
  Which left the matter looking very bad.

The neighbors, sympathizing with her grief,
  Formed a party to investigate the case.
So they dragged the stagnant water, and their
    search was very brief,
  Ere they saw poor Benny Rowland's livid face.
A bullet-hole above the ear was noticed in his
    head,
So before he struck the water he was evidently
    dead.

They reverently carried him and laid him in a shed,
  After washing from his form all muddy trace,
And a hoary-headed fisherman a deputation led
  Who broke the news to Marie with a tender-
    hearted grace.

The sergeant prowled around the hollow trunk,
  Discovering a recent trace of fire
About a narrow aperture that whimsically sunk
  Through the shell, 'twas partly hidden by a briar;
'Twas an easy feat to enter from the opening in the
    fork,
  Branches jutting out up which 'twas possible to
    walk
Like a ladder; at the bottom one could hear out-
    siders talk,
  By the slits, if anyone should so desire,
The knotty-grained interior, left nothing more to
    balk
The exit or the entry of an unsuspected spier.

The coroner impanelled fishermen
  To form a legal jury, and they found
A verdict that the body from the basin of the fen
  Had been murdered by a bullet, also drowned.
Over Marie's bitter sorrow I will draw a kindly
    veil,
As she mourned o'er the features gleaming rigidly
    and pale,
For somehow words are feeble to relate the touch-
    ing tale

Which hangs about the ivy-covered mound,
  Where for many days and nights there came an
    eerie, lonely wail,
    From the throat of Benny Rowland's faithful
    hound.

In the village, for a fortnight and a day,
  The popular excitement was intense ;
And the finger of suspicion seemed to point the
    bo'sun's way,
  Sustained by circumstantial evidence.
His foot-marks were measured all about the hollow
    oak,
And the day before he vanished there were words
    in anger spoke,
When the witnesses remembered how the bo'sun
    seemed to choke,
  When taxed with some mysterious offense,
And a surgeon proved the bullet, with a calm vin-
    dictive croak,
  To be fashioned by no English implements.

For it fitted a revolver Jane produced,
  From the room wherein he usually slept,
With a chamber lately emptied, that was owned by
    the accused ;
  This the council of inquiry wisely kept.
So the sergeant with a warrant for immediate ar-
    rest,
  On a charge of wilful murder, by the document
    expressed,

Went a hunting for the bo'sun, with a feeling in
    his breast,
    That no error in their logic could have crept.
Marie's tale was credited to wifely interest,
    And 'twas hinted there was reason why she wept.

His lordship was not home about that time,
    And no one was aware of his address;
'Twas a call of urgent business, so the story of the
    crime
    Could have only met his notice through the press.
The evening he went away the murdered man was .
    seen,
His lordship shortly afterward had crossed the
    village green,
To the railway; so the sergeant to the nearest town
    had been,
    The necessary warrant to possess.
If his lordship had been home his proper function
    would have been,
    As a justice, to have done it, and assist them more
    or less.

The rhymer went to Marie with a note,
    And she told him of the peril-laden cloud;
Her eyes were dim with weeping, so he read the
    message wrote,
    And reported the affair to the crowd.
Incipient rebellion was born among the crew,
Who scouted the idea that the charge could e'er
    be true;

They swore to back the bo'sun, till they took the
    vessel too;
    With adjectives profanely uttered loud.
The captain gained an inkling of the storm about
    to brew,
    As they went about their duties, heavy browed.

Then Marie came aboard for awhile,
    And they held a conversation when they met.
She handed him a bundle, with a melancholy smile,
    And their parting was a moment to forget;
She had brought her father's clothing for the fugi-
    tive to wear,
When he found it safe to meet her, by the haunted
    water, where
The murder was committed, none would pry upon
    them there—
    The innocent have nothing to regret.
At eleven in the evening she would wait a sudden
    flare,
    Of a lucifer extinguished after quickly flashing jet.

The captain pondered long upon the news
    And listened to the bo'sun's bonny bride,
Resolving to assist them by a very simple ruse,
    For he had the moorings dropped from off the
    side.
Repairs were now completed and the crew were all
    aboard,
The tanks were full of water, and provisions safely
    stored,

The sails were loosed and sheeted home, the zeph-
    yrs gayly poured,
    And they sailed down the river with the tide,
While a much bediddled sergeant on a jetty vainly
    roared,
    Looking anything but calmly dignified.

The banks widened outward as they went,
    They sailed like a witch across the bay ;
But they had to drop their anchor, for the lucky
    wind was spent,
    When the bo'sun pulled ashore, and ran away.
The intercepting cruiser searched the vessel fore
    and aft;
The captain met them kindly with a well-dissem-
    bled craft ;
But they left the vessel baffled, and the skipper
    suavely laughed,
    Inviting them to call another day.
Then he made the rhymer bo'sun, whom the sailors
    slyly chaffed,
    For the bo'sun's pipe is difficult to play.

Marie's husband donned poor Benny Rowland's
    clothes
    Finding they were not a bit too big ;
An artificial beard, after shaving I suppose,
    An iron-gray mustache, and bushy wig,
And the sharpest-eyed detective in the city would
    not guess,

That the venerable yeoman, in the evening ex-
    press,
Was a fugitive from justice; neither that he could
    possess
    Any coin in that dingy battered rig.
The skipper had provided him with money in ex-
    cess
    Of what was justly due him from the brig.

He quietly hired lodgings in a little wayside inn,
    Half a dozen miles across the moor,
Where he waited for a day or two, before he dared
    begin
    To ramble down toward the river shore.
One night he visited the oak, and in a narrow rift
Inside the hollow trunk he found a note, and
    hurried swift
To his lodging, where he gathered from the in-
    coherent drift,
    Of seeming empty phrases scribbled o'er,
That pursuit was reckoned hopeless, and she looked
    for him to lift
    The load from off her spirit, troubled sore.

He answered in an enigmatic key,
    In case it chanced to fall in other hands,
So that nothing should be known by any other one
    than she,
    That her husband had not fled to other lands.
And Marie walking daily where her father met his
    death,

Found the scrawl and read the meaning with a
    catching of the breath ;
For her faith was of the quality which never waver-
    eth,
    And she longed for the clasp of loving hands ;
Heeding little what the lawyer, or the sage old
    sergeant saith,
    Her instinct being all she understands.

PART FIVE.

The lord of the manor was young and bold,
And he lavished his ancestor's hoarded gold,
Till the coffers were dwindling lower and lower ;
So he cudgelled his wits to produce some more.
Mine host of the Anchor, the lawyer, and he,
Had joined in a treacherous gang of three
And woe to the gallant who went their way,
      For he came out lame
      From a desperate game,
Which frequently happens at play.

They noted the weight of the bo'sun's purse,
And the lord of the manor by tricks diverse,
Inveigled him into their cosey den,
To meet his associate sporting men ;
Who found with a feeling of blank dismay,
That the bo'sun had never known how to play.
But they cleverly made it a jocular theme,
      And he chose to remain
      With the beautiful Jane,
Who was lost in a perilous dream.

The lawyer had captured a casual friend,
Who was gently gulled as a great godsend :
He wagered his money with cheerful heart,
For a fool and his property ought to part ;
The morn was beaming in streaks of gray,
'Ere the revellers, rising, reeled away,
When the lawyer advanced the plucked pigeon a
     sum,
       With a generous air
       To purchase his fare,
And speedy return by the road he had come.

And the bo'sun crossing the river climbed
The gangway ladder, as clearly chimed
The hour of five, and the pipe rang shrill,
When the tars turned to, with a cheery will.
His lordship, merrily jesting, went
To the bo'sun's room, with serene content.
Arising late, when he chanced to find
       A revolver placed,
       With forgetful haste,
On a window-sill under the blind.

A handsome weapon of foreign make ;
So his lordship borrowed it, more to take
A shot as he rambled across the moor,
At a rabbit to see how it tumbled o'er.
But Jane diverted his first intent,
By saying the blacksmith's daughter went
To the haunted pool, in the eventide.
       The artful miss
       For the bo'sun's kiss,
Left never a scheme untried.

She noted his anger with great relief,
Believing her rival would come to grief;
Knowing his lordship willing to pay
For removing an obstacle out of his way;
His lordship, however, preferred to see
For himself, so he hid in the hollow tree,
Where a crevice had furnished an outlook fair,
  On any who strayed.
  And here he made
An excellent watch for the innocent pair.

That night he waited, without success,
For Marie was suffering great distress,
While the voice of her father in anger strong,
Was accusing her lover of treacherous wrong;
Who listened with never a harsh reply,
But a furious glint in his resolute eye.
Then he met poor Marie with heart downcast,
  And the lovers agreed,
  With a wondrous speed,
To be wed ere the following night was past.

On the wedding night in the hollow tree,
His lordship waited patiently.
The blacksmith hurrying thro' the night,
By the haunted pool arrived all right;
A murderous slowly formed idea,
In his lordship's mind arising clear.
If the bo'sun's revolver were picked up near
  Where the bo'sun died,
  'Twould be suicide,
And he had the revolver here.

If he missed his aim, 'twas a jest to scare,
Who he thought was the bo'sun waiting there;
Who probably would not care to wait,
In such an event, to investigate.
The moon was hidden in cloudy drift,
But he took good aim from the narrow rift,
Which steadied his sight on the shadowy head.
      A deafening bang
      In the silence rang,
And the blacksmith fell in the pool stone dead.

Half in the rushes arising rank,
Where a fagot had drifted against the bank;
So his lordship gave him a vigorous shove,
As a break in the clouds that careered above,
Illumined the scene with a ghastly glare,
When he saw who it was he had murdered there
And a picture was graven deep into his brain,
      Fated never to fade,
      Till his body was laid,
Not far from the grave of the man he had slain.

He floated out with his face thrown back,
On the drifted cushion of floating wrack,
As the fugitive beam of moonlight flew
O'er the face besplashed with a crimson hue.
On the long gray beard and the grinning teeth,
E'er the corpse sank silently down beneath;
And his lordship glared at the horrible scene,
      Then into the wood,
      O'er rocks and mud,
He wildly rushed to the village green.

'Twas deserted (the hour of eleven had struck)
Which he hailed as a token of excellent luck ;
Into the Anchor, and rang the bell,
Where brandy steadied his conscience well,
The weapon replaced where he found it first,
For he shunned it now as a thing accurst ;
Carried a bag to the midnight train,
      Staying away
      For a week and a day,
Since the outlawed bo'sun returned again.

His looks had suffered a marvellous change,
His manner was moody, and oftimes strange,
When the lamps were lit, if his eyes would close
The ghastly vision at once uprose ;
So he dranked and smoked till the break of day,
When the dire delusion passed away,
Which haunted the night with a horrible dread.
      When the sunlight fell,
      He would breakfast well,
Then he slept in the absent bo'sun's bed,

The window commanded a splendid view
Of the haunted pool, and the river too.
Each night he would peer at the stagnant mere,
Impelled by a feeling of mortal fear,
For every night as eleven clashed,
By the haunted water a bright light flashed,
Like the sudden gush of a pistol flame ;
      But floating back,
      No whip-like crack,
To his listening ears came.

One moonlit night, in a frenzied state,
He hurried forth at a headlong gait,
For it seemed to his highly distempered mind,
That a million demons pursued behind.
Disguised in a long, black, hooded cloak,
He rushed to the haunted pool and oak,
And there on the edge of the loathsome flood,
     With a smile so weird,
     And the long gray beard,
The ghost of the murdered blacksmith stood.

And the grisly arms in a vengeful clutch,
Encircled his waist, with a rigid touch,
A shuddering groan, and a maniac yell,
His lordship downward heavily fell,
And the phantom bending never spoke,
But tore off the shrouding long black cloak,
When the breeched extremities plainly showed,
     And the short cut hair,
     To a Gorgon glare,
When a baritone voice said, " Well, I'm blowed."

'Twas the cloak which misled the bo'sun's glance,
For Marie had bought by a singular chance
A similar garment, hooded too ;
The grass had deadened the heavier shoe,
So he gave the figure a fond embrace,
With a glistening smile on his bearded face,
But the agonized howl in the silent night,
     And his lordship's swoon,
     By the light of the moon
Made the bo'sun continue, " Well, blow me tight."

Over his shoulder like a sack,
The bo'sun carried him halfway back ;
When Marie came tripping along so gay,
Humming a rustic roundelay ;
Who, before the bo'sun had time to speak,
Gave vent to a vigorous female shriek ;
And the crew of a schooner stranded near,
      Came tearing along
      To right her wrong,
All chock full of valor and beer.

They gathered around with a threatening air
Demanding the bo'sun's business there ;
But his lordship awoke, and began to rave
Of a man he had shot, who had left his grave.
Then the bo'sun, in Benny Rowland's dress,
Sepulchrally ordered him to confess,
And the crew of the schooner all could swear,
      To the gruesome tale
      Which the trembling, pale,
And cowardly villain unfolded there.

It never occurred to the terrified wretch,
That his neck on the gallows would probably stretch,
Till they came to the Anchor and surged inside,
With the story of how the blacksmith died.
In the bo'sun's room he began to think,
But he steadied his palsied nerve by a drink,
And the lock as it sprung with an ominous click,
      Told a sinister tale.
      Of the county jail,
So the murderer made up his mind right quick.

His dressing-case lay on a closet shelf,
For the furbishing up of his valued self
After bibulous nights in the secret game,
And he peered therein by the candle's flame.
Certain documents took and burnt,
But what their nature could ne'er be learnt,
And a razor of genuine Sheffield blade,
     Exceedingly keen,
     With a shadowy sheen,
Beneath his pillow he carefully laid.

From a delicate phial of morphine pills,
Provided to settle his nervous ills,
Deliberate counting a threefold dose,
For his instinct told him the end was close;
Then closing the lid of the toilet-case,
He lifted it back to its usual place,
And his teeth set tight in a vicious snap.
     From sheer despair,
     Grown devil-may-care,
He silently grinned like a rat in a trap.

He stripped himself with unusual speed,
Got into bed, which was strange indeed,
Finished the brandy and swallowed the drug,
And settled himself in the pillow snug,
With a twist of the head till the jugular vein,
In the soft white muscle was beating plain,
His left hand holding the gleaming wedge,
     To the delicate skin,
     With a dreamy grin,
That a soul should ride on a razor's edge.

When the eyelids fell with a nerveless droop,
He made one feeble convulsive scoop
And a neat little nick in the sanguine duct,
While a curious noise in his windpipe clucked,
A shower of viscous crimson rain,
Went spurting out o'er the counterpane,
And his worthless soul winged out to——well,
     'Tis a bigoted haste,
     And atrocious taste,
To blather where any poor soul shall dwell.

The sergeant returned from the nearest town
With a warrant galloping hastily down,
For the lord of the manor was magistrate,
Which left the law in a ticklish state;
But the justice had, in an abstract sense,
Done justice, free from the vast expense
Entailed by the common judicial sieve,
     And the legal cliques
     Of quibbling tricks
Who manage by hook or by crook to live.

One good action, however, they did,
They found at the manor a document hid,
Which proved that a marriage had taken place
'Twixt the last of his lordship's reckless race,
And the fisherman's daughter. Who thus became
A highly respected and envied dame.
But she sent for the rhymer from over the seas,
     And the singular pair,
     Were united there;
So his banjo plunks 'mid the grand old trees.

Finding his lordship cold and stiff,
The sergeant went with a dubious sniff,
And finding the bo'sun down below,
He served the old warrant of which you know.
But the judge annulling the unjust ban,
The bo'sun became a most popular man,
And that night ere he slept in the blacksmith's cot,
      His wife and he
      Had the jolliest spree,
For the village apologized on the spot.

The smithy a capital warehouse made,
For a perfectly legal but scaly trade ;
His progeny toddles along to school,
Or go, which is wrong, to the haunted pool,
To cast a stone at the hollow tree,
Now full to the top, as it ought to be,
For the gloomy feeling the place inspired.
      And a favorite mark,
      On the gnarled old bark,
Is the rift where the fatal shot was fired.

And whither the Yankee vessel sailed,
Is a dubious point, where records failed.
The far-away port from whence she came,
Her tonnage, and gunnage, or Christian name,
Are gone with a glamour of mystery
Deep into the bowels of history.
The exact date of the famous ball
      Even, cannot be found,
      Which furnishes ground,
For a guess that I possibly dreamed it all.

www.ingramcontent.com/pod-product-compliance
Lightning Source LLC
Chambersburg PA
CBHW030556040726
47497CB00008B/2755